MARY UNDERWATER

SHANNON DOLESKI

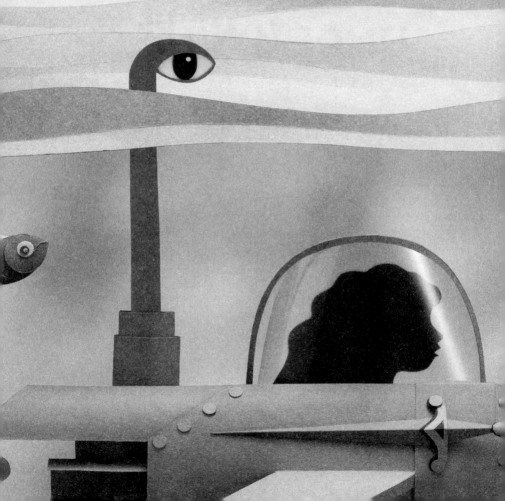

MARY
UNDERWATER

AMULET BOOKS • NEW YORK

Library of Congress Cataloging-in-Publication Data
Names: Doleski, Shannon, author.
Title: Mary underwater/Shannon Doleski.
Description: New York: Amulet Books, [2020] | Summary: Gaining courage from Joan of Arc, fourteen-year-old Mary Murphy navigates the waters of Chesapeake Bay in a submersible built with her friend, Kip, escaping the home where her violent father has just returned from prison. Includes facts about domestic violence and submersibles.
Identifiers: LCCN 2019033763 (print) | LCCN 2019033764 (ebook) |
    ISBN 9781419740800 (hardcover) | ISBN 9781683358145 (ebook)
Subjects: CYAC: Family violence—Fiction. | Ex-convicts—Fiction. | Friendship—Fiction. | Submersibles—Fiction. | Catholic schools—Fiction. | Schools—Fiction.
Classification: LCC PZ7.1.D637 Mar 2020 (print) | LCC PZ7.1.D637 (ebook) |
    DDC [Fic]—dc23

ABRAMS The Art of Books
195 Broadway, New York, NY 10007
abramsbooks.com

To June, Teddy, and Dwyer, my three little engineers

PART ONE

SUBMERGED

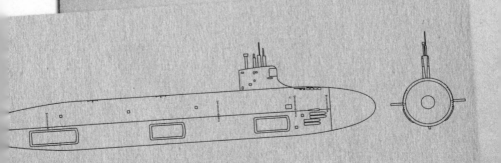

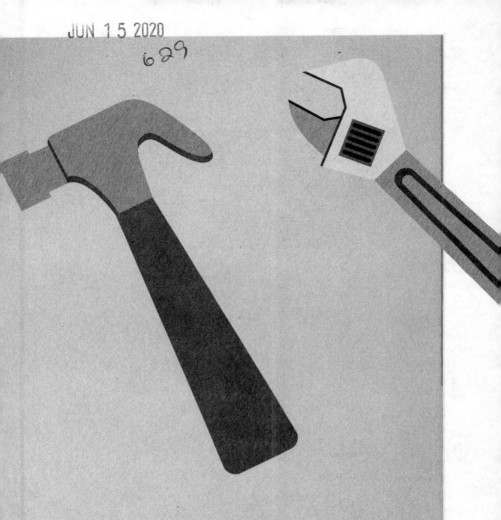

Anything that can go wrong, will go wrong.

—Murphy's Law

My dad is home, and anger has leaked back into the house. It rattles the walls and leaves bruises. If I'm not careful, it will pull me under. If I am careful, I can stay far away from it, sneaking with silent feet before anyone notices me.

I get dressed for school as quietly as I can while a battle rages in the kitchen. I press my hands to my ears, dulling the sound. Two weeks. He's been home for two weeks.

I pry my hands away and force shaking fingers to tie my dull black shoes and yank up my socks. When I stand, I pull on the hem of my jumper, the green-and-blue plaid faded. Sister Brigid has been after me since January about the skirt length, but two inches of kneecap appear no matter how hard I tug. "Our Lady girls do not show knee, Miss Murphy.

If you want that, go to public school. Please rectify this at once."

I can't fix it, so I haven't fixed it. At school, I avoid the nun at all costs.

From the kitchen, I hear a shout, so I hold my breath and wait. It's quiet for a second. Before anything else can happen, I grab my backpack, zip it shut, and slide out the back door.

Outside, I can breathe. The salty air of the Chesapeake is better than the suffocation of the Murphy house. My bike is propped against the porch, and I plant myself in the seat as fast as I can.

The Bay cuts up through the state. Like the water can't be contained, it carves rivers along the way, leaving ragged fingers of land. On the western shore, my island, Bournes, is a broken fingernail, surrounded by the Patuxent River on one side and Back Creek on the other. At the bottom of the island is the Bay and most of the houses.

I pedal north up the main street, the boardwalk to my left and shops to my right. The sun glints off the watermen's trucks parked at the marina. I veer right, where the island juts into Back Creek. Ahead of me is Our Lady Star of the Sea, a church the creamy color of a shell, with arched windows and doors. The low brick building behind that is the school.

As soon as I drop my bike at the rack, I unzip the tiny front pocket of my backpack and pull out the prayer card Sister Eu gave me in kindergarten. Joan of Arc, her hair short and dark, looks back at me. She's strong in gleaming armor, her sword raised high, the French battlefield in the background. I smooth the worn edges. I wish I were brave like Joan.

The entire time my dad was in prison, I didn't need the card at all. But now I press my eyes closed and whisper the words on the back. "I am not afraid."

I am not afraid.

I am not afraid.

I am brave and strong, my sword pointed high in the sky. Behind me is the Chesapeake Bay, the water gleaming in the April sunshine. I am not afraid.

When my heartbeat slows, I open my eyes. Before anyone can see, I slide the card back in the pocket, because thirteen-year-olds aren't supposed to play pretend. It's a weird thing to do. I know it's weird. But without Joan, I would drift away.

I follow the other students into Our Lady, the only school on the island. In the hallway, my friend Lydia waves. We might still be friends. I don't know. She's tall and pretty, and her black hair is in twists.

"Hey, are you coming over this weekend?" she asks me, opening her locker. She looks down the hall and smiles at someone.

"Maybe," I say. I haven't told Lydia about my dad being back. If I were braver, I would, but last time her mom called my social worker. If I stay away, it's easier. For everyone.

Lydia shuts her locker and turns around. "I want to show you my animation," she says. "It needs help." She makes these little sets in her room, dioramas with clay figures, and puts the short films online. They're beautiful.

"I'll ask," I say, knowing I won't.

"Okay. I gotta go!" She runs to catch up with Omar Wiley. I watch them turn into the Spanish teacher's classroom. If I'm not careful, I won't have a best friend soon.

In Mr. Fen's science room, I take my seat next to Kathleen Seton. Kathleen is weirder than I am. I think. She draws unicorns. Since kindergarten, she's only drawn unicorns, and worse, she talks to the paper while she's doing it. At least Joan of Arc really existed.

Usually, I like science. A lot. I even won the science fair last year in seventh grade. But lately, I can't shake off the fog of the morning. I stare at the front of the room while Mr. Fen talks.

My eyes drift past my teacher and out the window, to the slice of water behind the marina. No one is on the beach yet, but they will be soon, maybe in a week or two. Sometimes Lydia makes me go, but I don't like to. I never learned how to swim. Which is probably strange for someone who lives on an island.

"Mary!"

He shouts it like he's been calling me for a while. I meet Mr. Fen's eyes and fidget in my seat. It's a nervous habit.

"What would you say in that instance?"

"Umm . . ." I pick at my fingernail. "What instance, sir?"

The kids behind me giggle. I stiffen as my cheeks burn hot. I hate blushing.

"Were you paying attention, Miss Murphy?" Mr. Fen moves closer to me, inches away from the lab table. His shirt is as wrinkly as ever. "You know, if you spent less time staring at my tie, you would know the answer. Perhaps your grade would reflect that."

If melting into my seat were a possibility, I'd do it. And I wasn't even looking at his ugly tie.

"Mr. Fen, in her defense, your tie is exquisite. It's hard to pay attention when you wear clothes like that." Kip Dwyer. He is tall and freckled and has a gap between his two front teeth. When we were five, he mooned Sister Eu and everyone thought he was hilarious. He is. Sometimes.

When I hear his voice, I whip around, my two fat braids thumping against my desk. His eyes meet mine, and he winks. He's ridiculous. No one winks. He also doesn't need to rescue me from Mr. Fen. I refuse to return his smile and turn back toward the front.

To tune out my laughing class, I focus on an oyster recycling poster on the wall. A waterman with big boots holds up a bright yellow bucket. Restaurants turn in their discarded oyster shells. The lab on the south side of the island cleans them and then scatters them in the Chesapeake Bay to make new reefs.

"Oh, Mr. Dwyer, thank you for taking us off task." Mr. Fen shuffles a stack of papers and whistles us back to attention. Like we're dogs. I close my eyes and drop my head on the table.

"On that note, I'd like to hand back your tests from last week. Some of you should be very worried."

Everyone groans. Mr. Fen pretends he's all tough, but he doesn't yell at us about the groaning like other teachers would. Like the nuns.

When he gets to my table, he pauses. "I hope this was an exception, Mary," he whispers. I panic. Teachers whisper only when things are awful. He hands me the test facedown. Another unfortunate sign. When I flip it over, I see a big fat *F* scrawled at the top.

He starts to go over the hardest questions, but I can't pay attention. I want to escape. I want to ride my bike to the Cliffs, where I can breathe.

At the end of class, Mr. Fen stops me. "Sister Eu needs to see you in her office."

"Now? But I have French." A burning starts to bubble in my throat, and I'm afraid something will come out.

"Yes, now. I told her you can make it up on the project."

"The project?" I have no idea what he's talking about.

"Murphy, I've been talking about your physics unit for two weeks. You need to make a STEM project that explains one of the theories we've learned about. It could help bring your grade back up."

"Okay." Tears threaten to spill. "Can I go to the bathroom, Mr. Fen?"

"Sure," he says, picking up his coffee mug. "Just go to the principal's office when you're done."

∞∞∞∞∞∞∞∞∞∞∞∞∞∞∞∞∞∞∞∞∞∞∞∞

I bolt to the nearest bathroom. The fluorescent light flickers above my head. I look in the mirror, and shadows bounce on my face.

Get it together, Murphy. I splash water on my cheeks. I can talk to Sister Eu. She's just a person, just a nun. Just the daughter of a waterman, like me. It's not a big deal.

I adjust the waist of my jumper and try to make myself as presentable as possible. It's not easy. I'm a mess. My top is dingy, my knees are red beacons, and my socks keep falling down. I'm hardly Our Lady. Certainly not a star.

I walk down the hallway to her office, my footsteps the only sound. They make me feel alone. All of these people in this school, yet I am all by myself.

In the main office, the school secretary, Mrs. Rivers, uses her thumb to point me to Sister Eu's office. The door is shut. I press my fingers against the saint's card in my pocket. *I am not afraid.*

I prepare myself for the storm about to hit my shores. Board up my windows. Hide in the closet. And open her door.

We call her Sister Eu, like *you,* but it's really Eulalia. She talks like us, grew up on the island, and only came back after whatever school nuns go to and became the principal of Our Lady. In her black habit, she sits in her chair, waiting for me.

Across from her is a seat that might as well be an electric chair. I take my place and look down at my fingernails.

"Good morning, Mary." Her voice is always gentle.

"Sister." I fidget on the hard plastic.

"I assume you understand, after speaking with Mr. Fen, that we are worried, child."

Worried. Here we go. I am a crab plucked from my little perch, and she is watching my legs squirm.

I nod and jam my hand in my pocket and run my fingers along the card she gave me so long ago. I am brave. I am not afraid. I am Joan rallying the French troops against the English. I thunder up and down the line of men on my horse, a white banner fluttering at my side.

I am not Mary Murphy.

"Mr. Fen said you failed your test."

"He did?" My words squeak out.

She nods. "You were doing so well at the beginning of the year. Top five in your class."

Is that all she wanted? My stomach untwists. "Yes, Sister. I will take care of it."

Sister Eu sighs and folds her hands together. "I heard your father is home. Is that true?"

It's like she slaps me. Actually, I would prefer that. It would be over quicker. I need her to stop talking. "We have a big project. The eighth-grade physics unit? I can bring up my grade then. We have to make something. I think it can be anything STEM. That's science, technology, engineering, and mathematics. I always think it's mechanics instead, though. I like the engineering part the most—" The words roll out of me as fast as I can think them.

"Mary, child."

I stop and flick my thumbnails without looking at the nun, whispering, "My father is home, and it's crabbing season, Sister Eu." We need the money. Without it, my mom's job at the cannery won't be enough.

"It is," she says. "April already! How quickly the spring is moving." Her voice lacks concern. It's light, but I know what she's doing. That's what they always do, try to trick me into talking, and I will not be tricked.

"Is that all? May I be excused?" I am choking, and my eyes burn. I stand up, consumed, and look at my feet, which seem too big, too enormous to move without me falling.

She nods again and hands me a pass for Madame's class. "Mary." She blinks at me. Her brown eyes scan my face like she's trying to find the right words. "Good luck on your STEM project."

When school is finally over, I don't want to go home. I grab my bike and leave the island, trying to erase away the big fat *F* written in red ink that was my day.

Two bridges connect Bournes to the rest of the world, the older and smaller one to the north and the newer one to the east. I haven't crossed the new bridge yet. I leave the island and ride up to the Cliffs. A mile from school, the mountains of sand that are loaded with shark teeth and fossils wait for me. Access to the water, through a path in the woods, is public.

But the Cliffs and beach belong to the scientist community. Along the shore is a clump of little white cottages with screened-in porches and green lawns. They all look the same, and they're full of scientists who came to live on and study the Bay. Most of them are old.

The watermen, my father included, don't like them. The scientists aren't like the people of Bournes. They've got different ideas about the Bay. But I like them. They give me fossils and shells they find, and they don't mind when I come to their beach.

I can't ride my bike on the sand, so I leave it at the entrance of the trail. The sky threatens rain above me with dark, rolling clouds, but I keep going through the woods.

Under the cover of trees, the path is cool and quiet. It's low tide when I reach the water, and I'm alone on the beach.

For the first time all day, I can breathe. I let the safety of the Cliffs and the water cradle me. I sink, my knees scraping against oyster shells. I cry, my sobs loud. And the wind howls with me, in my ears, on my face, making my hair sneak out of my braids.

I yell at Mr. Fen. At Sister Eu. At my father. But mostly, into the storm, I yell at Mary Murphy.

I'm so wrapped up in myself, I don't see the person standing in front of me until he clears his throat. Kip Dwyer. Of course.

"Oh Lord," I say. I brace myself for a joke.

"Hi," he says. Instead of the dark blue pants and crisp white shirt of the boys' uniform, he's wearing jeans and a light blue T-shirt. His hair is blond and a little spiky. He clears his throat again. "Are you okay?"

I probably look like a wild-haired witch. I wipe my face and push back my loosened curls. "I'm fine."

"Okay, it's just, I was looking for shark teeth, and I saw . . ."

"You saw me crying."

"Yeah." I think he's grateful I answer for him. He digs the toe of his sneaker into the sand. Under his freckles, his cheeks pinken like he's embarrassed. How is that possible? I'm the one screaming and sobbing.

"I'm fine." I stare him down. Lydia tells me I look at people too intensely, my eyebrows straight black lines on my face. I'm probably doing that now.

"It looks like it's gonna storm," Kip says. "You might want to go home." Kip's family owns the marina. I don't like it down by their dock because all the watermen hang out there and talk about how funny Bobby Murphy is.

"You're not the only one who knows about the water, you know."

"Right." Kip looks out at the waves. "You sure you're okay? Fen was a jerk to you this morning and now . . ."

I wipe my nose one more time. "He was." And he wasn't. The more I think about it, the more I want to cry again, and I don't want Kip to see me. Again. I don't need more public embarrassment. "I'm fine, though. Really." It feels like I swallowed a marble. I need him to leave so I can be sad all by myself.

Kip puts his hand on the back of his neck. "When people say they're fine, they're usually not."

I'd rather he mooned me.

"I *am* fine."

He smiles.

"I am stupendous. I am wonderful. Is that better?"

"Very believable. Remember when we were in first grade and you used to come to the marina?"

"Yes." I don't know where he's going with this.

He grins, the gap thick between his two front teeth. "You made me sword fight with you."

I tuck my chin into my chest. "I know." *Please don't mention Joan of Arc. Please.* I squeeze my eyes shut and pray.

"You made me be English, and you were Joan of Arc."

"Yes!" I blurt.

"I liked that," he says. "We should do that again."

He wants to sword fight?

In his hand, Kip's phone dings. "My mom. I gotta go." He heads toward the path, then turns back and smiles again. In the wind, he yells, "I'll see you tomorrow, Mary Murphy."

And then I'm alone. I lie back in the sand and watch the darkening sky, then turn my face toward the rising waves. I could slip under them and kick until I popped up on the Eastern Shore. I could escape. I could start a new life.

If only I could swim.

Joan of Arc was born into war.

For almost seventy years, the French and the English had fought. England wanted French land. France wanted independence. But their king was unfit to rule. It was a time of great unrest.

When Joan was three, a great battle ensued in the north. The French were defeated by the English and the traitorous Burgundians in northern France. The loss was staggering and embarrassing. A treaty was signed, declaring the king of England the ruler of France.

France was devastated.

Joan lived on the border between the still-feuding factions. Although under Burgundian rule, her town was loyal to the French crown. They hated the English. They wanted freedom.

Fights and skirmishes broke out in her village. The roads outside of town were unsafe. Bandits and thieves attacked travelers. When the church bells would sound in alarm, Joan's father, the leader, would guide the villagers to the safety of a nearby castle.

The enemy could strike at any moment.

On Wednesday, I oversleep because my parents are arguing all night. I'm late to school, my twentieth tardy of the year. I burst into the science lab. The whole class turns to look at me, but no one's in their regular seats.

"Pick a partner, Mary," Mr. Fen says. He hands me a pink packet.

The STEM project. How could I have forgotten? If I can just get my grade up, everyone will stop asking me questions, and I can be a normal eighth grader.

Usually I work with Kathleen since we sit next to each other, but she's sitting on the other side of the room with one of the drama kids. So I stand there staring at my options, my heart still pounding from my rush to school.

"Fen, she can work with me!" Kip yells. "Watson is dead

to me!" He nudges his friend Ben Watson out of the seat to his left until he plummets to the ground.

Kip isn't exactly the best pick to help me salvage my science existence. I don't know what his grades are, but they can't be good. He barely pays attention. He has to stay for lunch detention in Fen's class almost every day. But I don't see how I have any other choice.

He grins up at me when I walk over to his table. *Please don't mention yesterday. Please don't ask me if I'm okay.* I sit and smack the packet down on the cool black tabletop. "Are you going to work hard?" I ask.

"Yes."

"Are you? Because I really need a good grade on this."

"I promise," he says. Kip slaps his palm to his chest, against the pocket of his white dress shirt. "I can't wait to do a project with you. It's gonna be great!"

I just stare at his freckles. Why? Why is he excited about this? I'm not sure, but at least he's not talking about yesterday.

I shake my head and turn my attention to the assignment. We could explain light reflection. We could manipulate heat energy. We could build an electrical current. And now I remember that, earlier in the week, Mr. Fen showed us projects from last year. A group had built a mechanical claw like at an arcade. That sounds like more fun than measuring light and shadows.

"I like building things," I say. "Do you?"

He leans forward. "I don't just like building things, I love building things. We could build Noah's Ark."

I roll my eyes and look at him. Some of the Our Lady girls think he's cute. Cute but immature. He never has girl-friends. "Why are you . . . ?" I don't understand. "This is the most we've talked since we were six, remember?"

"Six?" He frowns. "No, I definitely remember trying to hold your hand in fourth grade."

"That's not talking, is it?"

"No way, I was too scared to talk to you. Too pretty."

Is he making fun of me? I cross my arms. "Anyway, you can't just grab someone's hand. You should ask them first," I mumble.

"Okay, the next time I want to hold someone's hand, I'll ask."

"Good," I say. I have no idea whether he's talking about me or not, and I also don't know if I want him to be.

We are both very quiet. Too quiet. It's awkward, but my chest feels light for the first time in days. I scowl and read the instructions again. My best bet is to make something. Last year for the science fair, I made an oyster filtration system, and it was the most fun I've ever had in school.

"We're not building the Ark," I tell him. "But we could build a boat. Or a motor or something with water." I glance out the window at a big white fishing boat, buoyant and bob-bing on the surface. So vulnerable and exposed. One hole, one blemish, and it sinks to the bottom of the sea.

But there is one kind of ship that controls its buoyancy and spites gravity. One ship that can rise and rise and rise, even if it falls.

"We could build a submarine," I say. Like the display at the marine museum. There's a German submarine at the bottom of the Bay, the *Black Panther*. We learned about the wreck site. "We could make a model, like a remote-controlled one. I've seen videos online."

"Perfect!" Kip leans back in his chair and stretches his arms behind his head. "Fenster!"

Mr. Fen mumbles to himself and walks over to our table.

"What is it, Mr. Dwyer?" he asks, his voice dry. He rubs his head with his wrinkly tie.

"You're so strange, Fen, but I love you. I really do. That's not what I wanted to say." Kip clears his throat. "Sir, would you hold my hand? I promised Murphy I would ask permission."

Mr. Fen drops his tie and sighs. He ignores Kip and asks me, "Did you pick a project?"

I nod. "A submarine? Can we make a remote-controlled sub?"

"Good choice," our teacher says. "Oh, and I'll see you both for lunch detention," he adds, walking back to the front of the classroom.

I groan at the back of his crumpled shirt.

"Murphy's Law, Mary," Fen offers from his desk. "Whatever can go wrong, will." I've never heard of it, but it sure makes sense.

I glower at Kip. "You told me you were going to work hard."

"I am," he says. "I promise. I'll see you at lunch." He smiles, and one blue eye disappears into a wink. Like we are instant friends. Like Jell-O. Just add water.

3

At lunch, I go to Mr. Fen's room for detention, but I don't really mind. It's better than eating in the cafeteria anyway, where I have to pretend everything is fine to Lydia. Kip and I watch videos of other kids who have made similar projects, and then we look up submersible parts online. Submarines are used for war, and submersibles are used for science and discovery. Kip says his mom will probably pay for the parts if he's actually trying in school.

He makes me laugh twice. Once when he imitates Sister Brigid, and once when he falls out of his chair. I can't tell if it's an accident or not. Mr. Fen yells at him either way. After school, I ride my bike home smiling. I'm so distracted by the project and Kip that I'm not worried about the pickup truck with the dented front bumper parked in the driveway.

As soon as I step through the doorway, though, I know something is wrong. My stomach sinks. It's too early for him to be home from the boat. He should be on the water. Or at the Tavern. Not here.

Did Sister Eu call them? Did she tell them I failed my test?

She did. I know it. Or Mr. Fen did. My dad sits at the kitchen table, a beer can open in his hand. My mom stands behind him. They're waiting for me.

One step in, and I freeze. We all freeze.

The clock above the stove ticks loud in my ears.

I step backward to slip outside again, and when my heel touches the ground, my dad is up, the beer spilled.

I don't turn quickly enough. He's near me, his hand on my wrist, the only piece of me he can catch.

The fingers curl around my bone and squeeze, but I brace myself against the door and yank. Once. Twice. I'm free, slamming through the screen door and racing down the porch stairs.

I hide behind Mrs. Arlyn's house and rub my thumb along the mark, like I can wipe it away. Like I could wipe everything away. I hold my hand to my heart. I'm shaking, and the beat in my chest is frantic. A sob flies from my lips.

I fumble in my pocket and pull out Joan's card, wiping my palm over it. *I am not afraid. I am not afraid. I am not afraid.*

I close my eyes and blow out air slowly, deliberately. I am okay. I am not hurt, not really. It's been worse.

A door slams, and I glance around the corner of the house. My dad's truck drives away quickly, probably to the Tavern.

I give myself a few minutes, then shuffle my feet up the steps, my hand heavy on the wood of the railing. I sigh and open the door again. My mother sits at the table and runs her hands over her hair, frowning.

Susan Murphy used to have my hair–long, black, and unruly. Only, hers is sad now, limp and dull, the stress eating away at her until she's a living ghost. I don't want to be anything like her.

She speaks softly, barely above a whisper, even though she's loud when they fight. "I don't know why you have to upset him like that."

Her words slice through me. "I didn't do anything," I manage.

"You're failing science."

"It won't affect my scholarship. I won't fail science. I'm fine. I will be fine." I'm not sure who I'm trying to convince.

"Please don't mess this up, Mary. He's finally home. We need the crab money. If he goes back to prison . . ."

She says it like my science grade is the culprit, like failing a test is the problem. My mom shrugs her shoulders like there's nothing she can do about it.

My braids fly behind me as I run to my room to grab a jacket. When I leave the house, a glimpse back at my mom reveals nothing. I want her to do anything. Something. Tell me she's saving money to leave. Hug me. Tell me it's not my fault.

But she does nothing.

I race to the Cliffs, my feet pumping pure anger. It doesn't take me long to reach the path entrance. I drop my bike, then walk, my shoes making sloppy prints. I kneel in the sand and cry as the storm that never came yesterday finally hits our shores.

4

I throw myself into the project. Hurl my body against the walls of it. I meet Kip in the science lab every day at lunch. I start to meet him after school too. We go to Kip's house because the internet is slow at Our Lady. His sisters sit at the dining room table doing homework, and his mother brings us snacks. Their yellow Lab, Shrimp, sleeps on my feet, her nose pink and wet. It's loud, the noise from too many people talking at once, but always with smiles.

It is the opposite of the Murphy house in every possible way.

"What are you doing?" Babe asks me and Kip the third time I come over. Babe is two grades below us. Her real name is Barbara, but no one calls her that.

When she was a toddler, she played Jesus in the Christmas pageant and cried the whole time. She has freckles like

Kip. They all do, the Dwyer kids, like with each pregnancy their mom ate a different pen that exploded in her womb. None of them got their dad's red hair.

"Tell her, Murphy," Kip says.

"We're making a submersible."

On the table, we have an old fish tank and an empty soda bottle that will turn into the sub. Kip ordered a kit off the internet with a motor, servos, and a propeller. When I had asked him about it, he said his mom paid for it. Then he threw his pencil across the room at Watson and got us detention again.

I grab the bottle and float it on top of the water. "Subs have a pressure hull—usually really strong metal—so they don't get crushed under the pressure of the water. Like when you go down really deep in a pool and your ears hurt," I explain. "That's pressure. So subs need to be able to withstand that." Kip squishes his hands together.

I point to the cap. "Ballasts are pockets of air. When the sub dives, it's the ballasts filling up with water that makes the sub sink." I push the bottle under the surface. "And the sub moves up and down and side to side by flaps called diving planes and rudders." Two switches on the controller move them.

"That's boring." Monica is younger than Barbara. She has dark freckles and deep brown hair like her mother probably does when it's not dyed.

"Monica Frances Dwyer, you're being rude." Mrs. Dwyer is standing in front of the stove, the fan blasting noisily because she burned something. Her hair is a blond puff, and her skin is very tan like it's August and not May.

"Sorry, Mary," Monica says.

"It's okay," I tell her. I smile and scratch my scalp above my braid. "I don't think it's boring. I like it." I like it a lot. I like it more than anything. More than the filtration project I did last year. More than the Cliffs even.

And when Kip says he likes it too, I smile again.

The day before the presentation, I bounce my legs under the lab table. After Kip and I show the class our sub tomorrow, we won't have to work together anymore. It's been only three weeks, but I can't remember not being friends.

Mr. Fen goes to the cafeteria to get a sandwich, so we're alone in his classroom. I watch Kip peel a servo—the control that turns the sub left—off the flap and realign it.

Kip squints his eyes and sticks the servo on tight, his mouth pressed together in concentration. He jumps off the stool and runs to the sink.

He yells over the running water, "The controls work, but it's leaking." Last week, to store the battery, we cut the soda bottle around the middle and used tape and hot glue to seal it. "Should we add more glue?"

I pull on my braid. "No. It will keep leaking. It's weak there now, so we need to make something like a brace."

In Fen's supply drawer, I grab a spool of masking tape. I need the hard circle of the cardboard. Back at our table, I put the ring around the bottle at the leak. It just fits. I take it off again and fold up paper.

"What are you doing?"

"We need to reinforce it. Like if you broke your arm and had a cast." I roll the paper around the spool and stick clear tape over the whole thing. Then I tape that to the bottle.

When we put the sub back in the water, it doesn't leak. Kip says, "You're good at this, Murph."

I'm quiet at the compliment. I jam my hand in my pocket and run my fingers over Joan's card. "What are you doing after school?" I blurt out.

He looks at me sideways. "Are you asking me on a date? I knew you couldn't resist this physique. This charm."

My cheeks flare. "No, never mind." I stand up quickly, gathering my work to distract myself. *Is he making fun of me?*

"I'm kidding!" He laughs. "What do you want to do?"

"I was going to go to the Cliffs. Do you want to go with me?" I roll my eyes and look at the speckled ceiling of the science room. I wish I hadn't brought it up. It's a terrible idea. I want to curl up in my shell.

"Are we gonna make out?"

"We are not!" I rip my backpack off the table and turn to leave. He touches my elbow. It makes me feel light and bouncy.

"I'm sorry." He stands up. "I'm sorry. I was joking. I didn't really think that. Now, if you'd asked me to go to South Beach . . ." Kip winks. The south side of the island is where the high schoolers go. To kiss.

I suck in air. What was I thinking? Asking him was a terrible idea. I push my eyebrows down. "Never mind."

"Wanna look for shark teeth? I'll meet you by the bike racks? I need to be at the marina at six though. I'm on gas duty."

Clasping my books to my chest, I watch Mr. Fen walk back into the room. "I don't know now," I say to Kip.

Fen shakes his head. "Did you say 'gas duty,' Dwyer?"

"You're gonna mock me while Murph breaks my heart? That's cold, sir."

From his desk, our teacher laughs, opening his wrapped sandwich. "I didn't know you had a heart." He bites into his chicken salad and a glob of mayonnaise lands on his gray tie. I grimace.

"I do, and it beats entirely for Mary Murphy. You couldn't tell?" Kip grins, and steam evaporates off of me. *Stop it.*

"I think you overestimate your appeal," Mr. Fen points out.

"Are you an expert on women, Fen? You got a lady?"

"I don't 'got a lady,' Dwyer, but yes. I have a girlfriend."

He does? I wish she would address the wrinkled shirts with him.

"Do you love her as much as I love Mary?"

"Oh, dear Lord," I say. "I'm leaving." I'm sick of his jokes. I don't know what they mean, and I don't understand how he can make jokes twenty-four hours a day. It's unbearable.

The bell rings for fifth period, and I hurry to my locker. I catch Lydia's eye and she gives me a weak smile. She walks across the hall toward me. "Hey." She puts her hand on the locker next to mine. "Did you do the math homework? I swear, I don't get anything that man teaches."

"I did."

"Can you explain it like a human? Mr. Wisniewski is a calculator, I'm pretty sure."

I don't answer her, because Kip walks by and waves at me, but it's a loud wave, like noises come out of his fingers. Lydia grins at him. "What's up with you and Kip?"

I grab my English textbook and shut the door. "I don't know. What do you mean?"

"Are you together? I thought that might be why I haven't seen you."

I open my mouth to answer, but she says, "It's okay, I get it. Maybe we can double-date or something. Omar and Kip are friends. Then we can see each other."

Omar's dad works for the sheriff's department, so I don't want to do that at all.

"We're just partners on Fen's project."

"So, you just . . ." Lydia pulls on the short sleeve of her white shirt. Hers is crisp and bright. "Are you mad at me? Did I do something?" She tips her head to the side.

"No." My hand reaches for the card in my pocket. "No. I need a good grade on this project, that's all. But it's over tomorrow, and then I can hang out."

"Okay," she says. "I miss you."

My shoulders fall. I miss her too. So much. I just can't have her mom calling any social workers. If I can get a good grade on the project, then maybe everything will settle down, and we can be friends again.

The second bell rings, and now I'm late to Sister Brigid's class. I slap my hand to my face and run.

The nun marks me late, and I sit, scrunching up my face and thumping my pencil against the desk. When she tells us the page, I open my anthology, but I'm distracted. Why does Lydia think Kip and I are together?

Two rows ahead and to the left, he's sitting quietly because Sister Brigid won't let him be funny. *Do I like Kip Dwyer?* I like his freckles. And the gap in his teeth. I smile at the back of his neck where his hair meets his white collar.

I spend too much time thinking about it while Sister Brigid talks. At the end of class, the pope stares back at me from the poster under Sister's flag like he knows I'm thinking about a boy, and I slam my anthology shut.

5

At the end of the day, I dawdle. I get a drink, talk to Lydia and Kathleen, do anything I can to avoid going to the bike racks. Which is ridiculous because I asked him. And we've spent plenty of time together. This is no different.

Most of the other kids have left except for the athletes. It's bright out, and Kip is sitting on his bike seat, talking to Omar. Omar is slim, his dark hair neatly faded. He's on the soccer team.

Dragging my feet, I walk up to them with my hands on the straps of my backpack. I am uncomfortable. The sun feels too bright for May, and I think I'm getting a sunburn already.

"Hey, Murph!" Kip smiles at me. "You still mad at me?"

"I wasn't mad. You're just annoying sometimes." I push around tufts of grass with my shoe.

"That's nothing new, is it, Omar?"

"Annoying? Yeah. Pale too." They think this is hilarious and laugh until Omar says good-bye.

Then we are alone, and it is quiet. The sun roars above us, bright and warm, then dips behind a cloud.

He puts his backpack on. "You ready for our date? Can you keep your hands off me until we get to the beach?"

"You wish it was a date," I say. I stomp to my bike, snatch it from the rack, and take off toward the Cliffs.

"Murph with the jokes!"

〰〰〰〰〰〰〰〰〰〰〰〰〰〰〰〰〰〰〰

By the time I get to the trail, I'm out of breath. Fresh grass lines the sandy path, and I drop my bike. Kip falls in step behind me, jumping over a fallen tree. Once we get to the gritty shore, we look for teeth without talking. I stay close to the water, and Kip heads near the Cliffs. I scan, wipe away sand, and pocket anything worth saving.

I feel happy. Being close to the water makes me feel like I'm floating, the sun warming my skin. I think we'll get an A on Fen's project tomorrow. My grades will be fine. Maybe Lydia and I will be friends again.

Kip starts yelling from the Cliffs, and I look up. He races toward me, shouting.

In his hand is the largest shark tooth I've ever seen, half the size of his palm. He passes it to me, the tooth smooth in his warm hand. I know I blush when we touch, and I am mortified.

"I wonder how much I can get for this down at the marina. Or the retreat." He rubs his hand over his head, sweat trickling down his forehead, then lifts his shirt and wipes his face.

I look away. "You want to sell it?" I sit in the sand, smoothing my skirt under me.

"Yeah, what am I gonna do with it? I've got tons." He starts to take off his shoes, then his socks, and when he touches the button on his pants, I panic.

I squeeze my eyes shut. "What are you doing?"

"It's a million degrees out. I'm going swimming!" I hear him laugh, and it sounds like he falls in the sand before he reaches the water.

"Naked?" I whisper the word even though no one else is on the beach. I refuse to open my eyes to check.

His laugh is loud. "You think I'm naked? No matter where she is, Sister Brigid heard you and is praying."

"Shut up." I squeeze my eyes tighter.

"I have trunks on. For work. Promise."

I don't know if I should believe him. But I slowly open one eye, then the other, and sigh in relief at his bright yellow trunks. I'm thankful, though seeing him in shorts is just as uncomfortable. I might be the world's most awkward eighth grader. I don't know where to look or how to act. I've never been around a shirtless boy. Well, alone. And I'm sitting here, ridiculous, in my plaid skirt like it's the 1800s.

"What's wrong? Are you worried you'll fall in love with me if you look at me? 'Cuz I look like Thor."

I can tell he's grinning even though my gaze is safely on the water. "You do not look like Thor." Maybe if Thor had a little brother. A cute, annoying one.

"Then why are you being weird?"

Thanks. I finally look at him. "I don't know what to do."

"Neither do I." His face is sincere. He runs, splashing, farther into the Bay, and whoops. When the water's up to his waist, he dives below the surface.

A minute later, after he does a handstand, Kip comes out and stands above me, dripping water on my school shoes. "So, what do you think?" He flops down next to me, sand sticking to his skin.

I watch the waves roll in, my stomach imitating them. "What do you mean?"

"I like you, Murph," he says.

My brain feels fuzzy. It's confusing and wonderful. "I've never had a boyfriend."

"I've never had a girlfriend." He grabs his shirt and rubs it on his damp hair, drops of water landing on my arm. I lace my fingers together.

"Did you know Joan of Arc was supposed to get married, but she told her parents she didn't want to?" I blurt. Because it's quiet. Because my cheeks are on fire.

Kip laughs again. "That's such a weird thing to say."

"I'm nervous!"

He hops up and puts on the white undershirt the Our Lady boys are required to wear. He leans over and pulls me up by my hands. He doesn't drop them, and my palm is pressed warm against his. So warm. We are glued together.

No hint of a joke on his face, he asks, "Can I hold your hand when we walk back?"

I nod because I don't trust myself to talk. He can.

The morning of the presentation, I wake up to butterflies swirling in my stomach. Kip held my hand. I held *his* hand. But there's a fight in the kitchen because my dad is late for the boat. He's late for the boat because he was at the Tavern all night. I braid my hair in the bathroom and hear something crash on the kitchen floor.

My mom cries, and then the screen door slams. I close my eyes and breathe out, my mouth quivering. *Why today?* I need them normal today. *I* need to be normal today. I pull out Joan's card. *I am not afraid.*

A science presentation is not an impending army attack. I can do this.

Mr. Fen lets me in early and leaves to get coffee in the staff lounge. I pour buckets of water into Monica's bright pink baby pool, then sit at the lab table, my back straight and hands tight like a knot. Only my legs give away my nerves, bouncing out of control.

As each student walks in, I stare at the board, repeating the speech we've prepared. Almost everyone is in class. Except Kip. If I had a phone, I would text him.

He still isn't there for prayer or the Pledge, so I turn my attention to the door, willing him to enter. He said he would be here. He said he would work hard. I shouldn't have trusted him.

When he finally bursts in, I let out a huge sigh. Kathleen stares at me like I'm the weirdo even though she's the one talking to unicorns. Mr. Fen gives Kip detention, which he waves off. He pulls up a stool next to me.

"You miss me?"

I roll my eyes. "Glad you could make it."

"Oh, Murph, we're gonna destroy it. Babe puked. My mom had to clean it up. So disgusting. All over the stairs." He uses his hands for emphasis. "Just puke after puke after puke. Shrimp tried to eat it."

I glare at him.

"I had to walk Monica to school." He pats me on the hand. I wouldn't mind if he left his hand there, even if he is talking about vomit.

"Dwyer, stop discussing bodily fluids and get up here to present," Mr. Fen barks.

"Of course, Fen, sir. I'm so excited to tell the class about submarines."

"You're just excited to talk for twenty minutes without punishment." Fen looks at me. "Ready, Mary?"

We're getting an A. I can feel it. And by some miracle, I don't pass out from nerves. Kip doesn't need notes and entertains everyone while I flip the switches on the controller. Fen only has to yell at him once during our presentation.

When we're finished, I sink back into my chair and bury my head in my arms. We did it. We did well. I won't fail science. But an empty feeling hovers in my chest. It's over. In a few weeks, school will let out for the summer, and I'll be held captive in the house on Bleecker Street. I'd rather be in this science lab for lunch detention.

"What's wrong, partner?" Kip asks me. "We were amazing!"

I tip my head to look at him, the table smooth like the inside of an oyster shell against my cheek. I want to tell him. I want to tell him about my dad. The words creep to the tip of my tongue, but I stuff them back down. "Nothing."

"Hey, I have to work at the marina, but can I walk you home after school?"

"Why?" The Dwyer house is right behind the church. My house is a mile away.

"Mr. Dwyer! I am very aware your assignment is complete, but Kayla and Olivia would like to present theirs now. Is that okay with you?" Mr. Fen yells.

"Yes, sir. My deepest apologies, ladies. I can't wait to hear about kinetic energy. Tell me all about it!" He immediately turns back to me and opens his mouth. "How come you never get in trouble?"

"Because I'm so sweet."

He laughs, and Fen shoots him a look.

Kip leans in closer and whispers, "I want to walk you home so I can see you, Murph. I thought that was kind of obvious."

"Oh," I say. He does? I feel my cheeks flush. "Okay."

"Okay."

Joan prayed in the fields when she tended to the sheep, under the bright blue sky, and in the chapel in the woods under the old oak trees. She lit candles and sensed the angels and saints all around her.

She first heard their voices when she was thirteen. In her father's garden, the sun warm, Michael, defeater of Satan during the war in heaven, appeared. He called her name, his sword at the ready. Though she was terrified, the saint soothed her.

And then more visited. Saint Catherine. Saint Margaret. They came to her garden often and spoke to her.

Joan prayed about the visits. She spoke to the village priest. She fasted.

And then she knew what they wanted.

What her whole village prayed for.

Freedom.

She would seek the dauphin, the son of the late French king. She would encourage him to lead France. She would make him crowned king.

She told only her priest.

When she was fourteen, her parents decided she should marry. They picked out a groom and announced it to the church members. But Joan didn't want to get married. She knew she had different plans.

Vowing never to marry gave her the courage to tell those around her about her calling. She would fight for her country's independence.

The young maid from the forest of oak trees would save France.

7

All day, I'm distracted, a different distraction than my parents. At lunch, I miraculously don't have detention, so I sit with Lydia in the cafeteria and nod along, barely paying attention, as she tells me about an argument between two of the band kids. And when the bell rings at the end of the day, I hurry to the bike racks.

When Kip comes outside, he's laughing with some of the other boys. He says good-bye to them and raises his eyebrows at me. "Murph! Where have you been all my life?"

"I saw you an hour ago." But I smile.

Kip doesn't have his bike. He unbuttons the top button of his shirt and rolls up his sleeves while I pull my bike out of the rack.

I walk it, my hands on the bars, and we are both quiet and awkward. Kip is a lot different, less confident, when he doesn't have a whole classroom to impress or a teacher to tease. But I like him more like this. I bite my lip, thinking about how he sword fought with me when we were little. I accidentally knocked him off the dock.

"Buddy was at the marina yesterday," he says.

"Oh yeah?" I don't know why he's talking about Buddy. Buddy is an old waterman who doesn't go out on the boats anymore. He gossips at the marina and hangs out on the boardwalk, talking to anyone who walks past.

And then I wonder how much Kip knows about the rest of the island because of the marina. About my family. Does he see Robert Murphy? Does he think he's funny? Does he know he was in prison? I clear my throat.

"He said there's a scientist in the retreat, a guy named Ford something. Wait, Ford Wallace. Or Wallace Ford?" A scowl forms under his freckles. "Either way, there's a guy there who built submarines for the Navy." He rubs his neck and says, "I don't know what we could do with that information, but I thought you'd want to know it."

"A man who built subs? Lives here?"

"Yeah, I think he still does. You know Buddy says stuff that's half true, so I don't know, but it sounds like he still builds them, like, for rich people. Like weird billionaires with lots of time on their hands."

I stop walking and look out at the Bay. People build real submarines? I guess I knew that, but someone in the Scientists' Retreat builds subs? He's not in a nameless video on the internet. He's right here, in the county.

I shove my hand in my pocket and pull out Joan's card. *I am not afraid.* And the other half of the quote, the phrase I've never said. *I was born to do this.* Because I've never felt like I was born to do anything. Joan of Arc was destined to save France. And me? Born to survive, maybe. But a thrill runs up my spine like nothing I've ever felt before. "We could make one."

Kip keeps walking ahead of me until he realizes I'm not beside him. "What? A sub?" He comes back and takes my bike by the handlebars. "Like a real sub?"

I nod. A real sub. A real sub that could leave the island.

"You want to make a real submersible that goes under the water?"

"Yes, that's what a sub does." And I want to keep working with Kip. We're a good team. Mr. Fen stopped me in the hallway and told me we'd gotten a ninety-eight on the model. I want to keep going.

"Murph, you think we, you and me, the two of us, can make something that survives underwater?"

"Yes." I blow out a long breath and smile. I do. Across the water is the Eastern Shore. We could go there. I've never been. I squeeze my hands at my side, the card tucked in my palm. I don't know how we'll do it, but I think we can.

Kip leans the bike against him and folds his arms tight to his button-down. The blue of the bike is faded from the sun. He shakes his head. "Well, I'm not going in it. Too scary."

"Oh." He doesn't want to. I tilt my chin down. *What was I thinking?*

"But I think you should probably realize by now that I would do anything to spend more time with you, so yes, I will help you build a real sub. Even if it is a death trap."

I drop Joan in my pocket and run my hand over the fabric of my dress, a rush building inside me.

I will dive. I will sink. I will surface.

I will get off this island.

8

The driveway is empty when I say good-bye to Kip. *Thank you, Joan.* Mom must be at work at the cannery, and my dad must be on the water. I have the house to myself.

In my room, I draw submersibles. I look over the notes I made about the model. Basically, it will be the same because we need the same components. I'll need to be able to breathe and see. At my desk, I scowl at the paper.

Where am I going to go? I know we have a map of the Bay somewhere, and I search the kitchen and the living room. I find a depth chart, folded tight in a bookcase. I spread it across my desk. Seven miles. I have to survive for seven miles.

I can do that. I can survive almost anything.

The hull can't be made out of a plastic soda bottle, of course. It has to be something stronger, able to sustain pressure, even though the Bay isn't deep. I saw one video online with a kayak. The man was able to paddle out into deep water and then convert it into a sub. I don't have a kayak. I don't have much of anything. I glance around the bare walls of my bedroom.

Maybe Kip has something at the marina. Huge barns near the docks are full of boat equipment. At least there were when I was six. Maybe there's a propane tank. My heart pounds. That would work, if I can fit in it. Propane tanks are pressurized.

I'm jotting down the words "propane tank" when the phone rings. I run to the kitchen and grab it.

"Susan?" a voice says. "Wait, is this Mary?"

I don't recognize the voice at all. "Yes."

"Glad I caught you. This is your aunt Betty."

"Hi." I don't know much about my mom's sister, Betty. I know she lives out west. I know she sends me cards on my birthday and presents that my father thinks are "too California."

"I just moved back in town and was hoping you'd meet me for lunch."

Why does she want to see me? What's going on? I haven't seen her in years. I don't even remember what she looks like.

"Mary? Are you still there?"

"Yes, I'm here." The last time I saw Betty was in third grade, when things were really bad. Is this about the science test? It was one test. I'm passing. I'm fine.

"Noon on Saturday? Does that work for you? The Harbor Restaurant?"

I nod. "Okay."

When I hang up, I bend the pencil in my hands until it snaps in half.

I don't mention the phone call. Not that my parents ask me about anything, but I want the meeting with Betty to be a secret. Saturday, when I leave the house, no one's home to ask me where I'm going.

My hair is braided as usual, but I wrap it around my head like a crown to keep it off my back in the heat. I'm nervous and sweating in Lydia's hand-me-down purple shirt. I don't go out to eat much, especially with long-lost relatives I barely know.

The Harbor Restaurant is close to my house, so I walk. On the boardwalk, I see neighbors walking dogs, taking pictures of the new bridge, and buying ice cream at the marina. Mrs. Arlyn waves and says hello.

When the restaurant comes into view, I scowl. *What does my aunt want?*

"Mary!"

Turning my head, I see a bunch of Our Lady kids, Omar and Lydia and some ninth graders, standing in the shade of the gazebo where they hold concerts on Friday nights. Lydia runs over to me, smiling. Until last year, she had braces that she hated. She'd smile behind her hand. Not anymore. Her smile is bright and confident. "Hey! Wanna hang out? We might see a movie."

"I can't," I say. I shove my hands in the pockets of my jeans that feel too hot for the weather.

"Okay," she says, but her voice has changed. She frowns. "Do you have plans?"

I shift on my feet. "Yes."

Lydia waits for me to explain. I can see it in her wide eyes, but I don't know what to tell her. I want to. I want to tell her that I'm worried about why I'm meeting my aunt, who I haven't seen since, well . . . But I can't.

She looks down at her feet. Black sneakers that are scuffed on the toes, but not the same way mine are. Her scuffs are intentional, like she couldn't wait for the shoes to wear down. "I don't really feel like we're friends anymore," she whispers.

"We are," I say, but my voice bobs.

"Friends tell each other stuff."

"I know." Tears fill my eyes. "I know they do." In her room is a framed picture of the two of us in diapers. I gave it to her when she turned twelve.

"It doesn't feel like you know that."

I've been shot. I've been hit by an arrow. Lodged in my chest, the feather quivers with my breath.

Joan was hit too. She pulled the arrow out herself and returned to battle.

Not me. I just run. I run away from my best friend of twelve years, crying the whole way to the Harbor. My stomach aches as I reach the front of the restaurant, where the hostess takes down names. I wipe my eyes one more time before I say I'm there for a Betty Vernon.

She brings me around tables of laughing people, mostly tourists, and my chest burns. I'm a terrible friend. Why couldn't I just tell her where I was going?

The new restaurant smells like seafood and lumber. The hostess drops me off in front of a woman with shoulder-length black hair, pinned back at the sides, and large plastic glasses.

She looks me up and down. "So, you're Mary, huh?" My mother is younger, but Betty looks rested. Betty looks sophisticated.

I nod. "Yes, ma'am."

"Well, sit down then. No need for ma'am. We're blood after all."

When I sit, I pull down my T-shirt and run my thumb over the card in my pocket.

"Call me Betty," she says. "I'm not exactly welcome at your house because of my wife, but since I'm back, I thought we could see each other more."

Her wife? No, my dad would not like that.

"You look like your mom," she says, a slight smile on her lips.

The waitress takes our drink order, and behind my aunt, I watch the cars on the bridge. It's so tall—Navy ships fit underneath—and during the air show, pilots fly between the Bay and the bridge. Before it was built, if you wanted to get to the other county, you had to drive an hour north.

"Your mother called me." Betty is deliberate in her speech, gruff. I wait for more information. "Bet your dad liked that." Her laugh is deep and gravelly like stones rolling around in her stomach.

I stay quiet.

"You're having a hard time in school, your mom says."

"I'm fine." I don't want to talk about Our Lady.

"What does that mean? Explain." Betty folds her hands on the table and scrunches her brow, the same expression I make.

"I'm passing."

"Just passing is no way to live a life."

I don't say anything. She's right.

"I guess it's pretty hard to work on school when they're carrying on all the time. You would think they'd have every-thing argued out of their systems by now."

Does she think they only yell? There's a lot more than yelling.

Betty leans in. "That's why you weren't doing well?"

I squirm in my chair and play with the straw in my drink. "I don't know."

"Mary, if we are going to know one another, you must be honest. That's how I am. I won't fraternize with someone who doesn't speak their truth." She nods at me.

I look down at my lap. "Yes," I whisper. "That's why."
It feels disloyal, telling. But it also feels really nice. A layer
of armor is torn from my chest. Without the weight, I
can breathe.

"I can't undo thirteen years of bad parenting, but I'll do
my best. That's for certain."

I smile at her and feel immediate relief. Betty is nothing
like my mom. Nothing like my dad. But I still don't know why
we're meeting, and that is a small shard of glass stuck in the
bottom of my foot.

9

When we say good-bye, I head to the marina. The crowd of
kids under the gazebo is gone, and my heart aches. I don't
know how to make it better with Lydia. I don't know how to
fix our friendship.

The paint on the sign above the marina is flaking, and
the door dings when I open it. I haven't been here in years.
Kip's sister looks up and smiles at me. I give Barbara a little
wave, and she tells me he's out on the dock.

Kip has his back to me, talking to a man fueling his boat.
The waterman laughs and gestures at me. Kip turns and
smiles. "Murph! Did you come to sword fight?"

I shake my head, smiling. He's so ridiculous.

"Excuse me," he says to the waterman. "I gotta talk to
my lady."

"I'm not your anything," I say. But I have to force a straight face. I look out at the water and squint my eyes, scanning for my dad. "Can we work on the sub?"

"I can't wait! Let's build you a death trap."

Except we have no idea what we're doing. Or where to start. In between gassing up boats, we watch videos on Kip's phone. I scowl at the screen as a man pulls a hatch down on a homemade sub. A tube for breathing runs from the sub to the air. It doesn't seem safe.

I fold my arms. The more videos we watch, the more worried I get. There are so many variables. I didn't think this through. Do I want oxygen in the sub? Do I trust a tube to provide enough to get me across the Bay?

∾∾∾∾∾∾∾∾∾∾∾∾∾∾∾∾∾∾∾∾∾∾∾∾∾

For a week, I split my time between Kip at the marina and Betty. On the weekend, I volunteer at the library in North Beach where she works, stacking shelves after kids yank the books off. She gives speeches. About the president. The election. The patriarchy. She says, "You can only save yourself in this life." Everything is the opposite of what I hear at home.

When she drops me off at my house on Bleecker Street, I head to the marina as fast as I can.

On Sunday, after a week of watching videos and trying and failing to do anything with the propane tank, I tell Kip, "We should go visit that man."

"Okay," he says. "Dad said his name is Ford Wallace. Let's ask for help."

∿∿∿∿∿∿∿∿∿∿∿∿∿∿∿∿∿∿∿∿∿∿

We ride our bikes to the cottages of the Scientists' Retreat. They're small and white with screened-in porches full of patio furniture. A few have grills and firepits. Some have gigantic telescopes, and more than one looks like a junkyard, with car engines and motorcycle parts in the driveways.

I point to the closest one, a number seven next to the screen door, and look at Kip. I don't know any of the scientists individually, only as a group. "We could ask here?"

"You're in charge." He waves me toward the door.

I take a deep breath and knock. A man with long gray hair and wrinkled skin the color of driftwood opens the door. "Namaste, my brother and sister." He's shirtless and his pants billow. I hear Kip hold back a laugh.

"We're looking for Ford Wallace. Could you tell us where to find him, sir?"

"Is everything copacetic?" he asks.

I frown. "I don't know what that means."

"I think it's hippie for good." Kip smirks, and I roll my eyes, hoping he's not offending the man.

"Nothing bad," I tell the man. "We just had some submarine questions." It takes all my control not to yell at him, demanding to know which cottage belongs to Wallace.

"Cool, cool," he answers. "Cottage twelve. Hey, do you

kids like yoga? I've got some pamphlets in here." He turns back into the house, the door open.

"No, man, we're good. Thanks for the help!" Kip says, hurrying me along by the arm.

I stop and watch him walk down the stone path to number twelve. He touched me, and I know he's done it before, but it was warm and nice. I'm not used to it.

"You coming?" he calls back to me. His freckles are as bright as his grin. "You scared?"

I am not. I was born to do this.

10

Cottage number twelve has the messiest yard. Three ancient lawn mowers but no real lawn. A blue boat seat not attached to a boat. An anchor. I take a deep breath and knock.

After a minute, I knock again. I look at Kip, and he shrugs. We can hear movement and something that sounds like furniture being dragged across the floor. Or a dead body.

We wait. I'm curious and impatient. I keep exhaling loudly, like the more air I push out, the more relaxed I'll feel, but it isn't working. I try convincing myself that we are asking for help, so be patient. That's not working either.

"I'm coming!" we finally hear. "Just a minute."

A little man with ruddy cheeks answers the door, breathless. "I'm sorry," he says. "So sorry. How can I help you?" He nudges a stack of books with his bare foot to open the door wider.

"I'm Mary Murphy, and this is Kip Dwyer. We're looking for Ford Wallace."

He drops his arm from the door and grins with his bottom teeth. "Well, you're in luck, young lady, because I happen to know him quite well." His voice is happy and southern, a stronger accent than I've ever heard. Sticky.

I want to push down the door. "Could we speak with him?"

"Well, let me check." He says the last word like it's stuck to the top of his mouth. He pokes his head behind the door, so we can see only his body. "Ford Wallace, can you talk to these beautiful young folks?"

I blush, and he pops his head back. "I can! Because I'm Ford Wallace!"

He's so weird. I can't even look at Kip because I know if I do, I will laugh.

Wallace lets us in, and we dodge piles of paper, books, and pieces of machinery. He motions for us to sit, after removing an empty oyster can and smoothing out a fuzzy cushion.

"Well, what can I do for you sweet little teens?"

I smile and let my shoulders relax. Sometimes I'm nervous around new men, but it is immediately clear that Wallace is not Bobby Murphy.

"*You* were in the military?" Kip blurts, surprised. I shoot him a look.

"Why, yes. I was. Granted, I was much handsomer and younger then." He laughs, a nice easy one that makes his gray eyes disappear. Wallace is small and fine-boned like a bird. Kip's right—he doesn't seem like the military type.

He's wearing an untucked button-down shirt and rolled-up khakis. He seems completely content with himself, and I'm envious.

"That's kind of what we want to talk to you about," I start. "Kip and I built a remote-controlled submarine." I fill my lungs. "And we're trying to build a real one."

"You two?" For a moment, he watches us without talking and without expression. And then his face clouds.

The change makes me whisper. "Yes, sir."

"How much money do you have? Do you have a backer? How about a lawyer?"

I shake my head and scowl. "I don't have any money." It burns to say that in front of Kip. I plunge my hand into my pocket.

Ford Wallace laughs. "I can't do much with no money. And a lawyer. I can't help without one. Submersibles are illegal, so you need representation if things get contentious."

"I don't know a lawyer." I also don't know what "contentious" means.

Wallace is not smiling anymore, and I wish the nice, weird man who answered the door would reappear. Kip clears his throat and stands up. "Thanks for letting us in, Mr. Wallace. We can let ourselves out." He walks to the door.

I follow him, defeated. Tired. Tired from everything. I assumed Wallace would help, for some reason. And now I just feel exhausted.

"Wait," Wallace says. He turns and leaves the room. And for a moment, I feel hope. I look at Kip, and he shrugs.

Wallace comes back with the largest book I've ever seen. He hands it to me, and I falter under the weight. *Building Your Own Submersible* by Ford Wallace. The cover is a photograph of Ford as a young man sitting on top of a home-made sub.

"Does this mean you'll help?" I ask.

"Oh no," Wallace says. "It's so I have a clear conscience, my dear. Good luck."

Good luck. We both know I'm destined for failure.

"Okay, Murph. Let's go," Kip says. He takes the book from me, and I walk out the door behind him. The screen door bangs against the cabin.

Outside, Kip and I walk through the path from the Cliffs. I don't want to speak.

"So, he was different than I expected," Kip eventually says.

I nod. The sun is almost gone, and the air is so heavy, I can almost drink it.

"I mean, his voice, you know? What kind of accent is that?" Kip keeps cursing as his feet hit the sand. "Could you spend a minute with him in a submarine? With that voice, Murph?"

I can't even answer him. I am lost. Floundering.

Kip stops. "What?"

I kick the sand with my shoe and look at the shore. "Nothing." I walk ahead of him.

"Don't let him bother you. We'll make one. We don't need his help."

"Do you think so?" I pause and don't face him. "I was stupid and thought he would help."

"Who cares what that guy said? You stick to things, and I will do whatever you want."

"I do?"

Kip grabs my hand with his free one and locks our fingers together. His palm is warm, and I believe him. I smile down at our hands. God, I like him holding mine. I think it's my favorite feeling in the world.

"Worst-case scenario, I make you a submarine sandwich."

I drop his hand and laugh. "Oh Lord, you are so ridiculous."

For a minute, I feel light. But when I get home, I put the book on my desk and stare at it. Ford Wallace doesn't want to help me. And why would he?

11

"Psst, Murph."

I roll over and groan.

"Murph!"

Sighing, I open my eyes.

"Murphy! You up there?"

I hear the whisper, which is really more of a yell, and realize that someone is waking me up in the middle of the night.

I push back the sheet and sit up. The sky is still black when I pull open the curtains.

"Hey, it's Kip!" He waves at me, the top of his head at the bottom of the window.

"I see that. What time is it?" I feel groggy. And grumpy. Grumpy about being woken up and grumpier about Ford Wallace.

He holds up his phone, the light so bright in the dark, I squint. "1:27. Come out here, please. I gotta show you something."

"It's the middle of the night."

His face is tiny squares of a window screen, one freckle per box. "I was dying for some Joan facts. Where else would I get them?"

"Google." But I'm trying not to smile.

He beams at me, and his blond hair looks fluorescent under the one streetlight on Bleecker. We haven't been alone since Sunday, when Ford Wallace rejected me. "Okay, it's really about the sub. Let's go! I've gotta go to work at six."

I peek at the driveway. Dad's truck isn't parked out front, so I step quietly down the hall. When I get to the screen door, I try to not let it bang against the frame.

Kip's waiting for me in the grass. It's hot and sticky and humid. Up and down the street, I watch for lights.

"You look pretty, Murph. Never seen you with your hair down."

I look at my bare feet. At night, I take my hair out of my braids because it hurts to have them tight while I sleep. But during the day, I like them. They make me feel in control.

Kip reaches over and grabs a strand. My heart scrambles, and I gasp. I probably shouldn't be standing in the grass in the dead of night with a boy who touches my hair. Sister Brigid will know. I swat his hand away, but he grins anyway.

"Stop."

"I will do whatever you say." Kip winks and takes a seat in the grass, patting a spot next to him.

I join him, the grass soft against my feet and legs. "You need to stop that winking business."

"I only wink at you."

"I doubt that."

"I swear!" He puts his hand on mine. "I actually need to tell you something else." He takes a deep breath. "Your eyes are pretty. Like silver almonds."

I panic, jumping up. After midnight with the boy I . . . well, I don't know. The boy I like. That seems dangerous. Handing him my heart, the one beating wildly against my ribs, seems dangerous. And impractical.

"That's what you needed to tell me? Okay, thank you. I will see you in school on Monday."

"Murph. I broke into the Navy base."

I turn. Breaking into a military base has to be a crime punishable by death, I assume. I pull on the ruffle at the bottom of my nightgown and try to bring it down past my knees. The pink fabric is worn and frayed in spots. "What does that have to do with me?"

"I want it to be a surprise, Murph! Please come with me across the bridge. It'll be worth it, I promise!" Kip starts moving across the front yard, and I see the curtain move in Mrs. Arlyn's house, the old gossip. Why is she awake now?

I want to follow him. I want to sneak across the grass into the dark night.

"Wait, Kip! I'm not even wearing shoes. Hang on."

I run back up the steps to grab my tennis shoes and catch a glimpse of myself in the mirror in the living room. I see what Kip sees. I look happier with my hair down, and also a little like a witch. I like it.

Outside, I feel happy and mischievous, and my cheeks hurt from smiling. "I'm ready."

"Looking a little devilish there, Murphy."

"I feel a little devilish." I pull my hair off my neck.

"Good," he says. "Maybe I'll get a kiss."

I panic again and only manage a loud, nervous laugh that lasts a lot longer than a normal laugh is supposed to last.

"Murph, we don't have time for making out. How many times do I have to tell you? I'm in a hurry."

Quietly, we race the five minutes to the bridge, stopping when we get to the concrete. A warm wind blows, making the bridge sway gently like a hammock. I glance over at Kip. Is he scared too? It looks like there aren't any sides, like a car could drive an inch to the side and plummet into the water.

"I've never been on this before," I say. My fingers tingle.

"There's a walkway." He points. "Not a big deal."

"I don't like that it's moving." I know why it sways. It's like we learned in our physics unit. If it were rigid, it would break. Shatter like glass into the twinkling water below.

My mother is terrified of the bridge, even boycotted it during the planning stage at the county board hearing years ago. I don't think she's driven over it yet.

"You can sneak out, but you can't walk across a bridge?" Kip asks.

"That's because I hate my parents," I say. The words slip off my tongue, out of my control.

"Yeah, me too. My dad's been cheating on my mom for years, and I have to keep it a secret from Babe and Mon so they don't find out. My parents are like two robots."

"Oh." The Dwyers seem so perfect. I had no idea. "I'm sorry," I tell him.

He shrugs, but he's tense under his T-shirt. If I were braver, I'd hug him. "That's okay. Wanna talk about yours?"

Something about the dark makes me think I should. It would feel nice to let it out, let down my guard, and for a second, I think about allowing the words to leak out of me like tears. "Aren't we on a countdown? Don't we have to go see something?"

I march up to the bridge and take a confident first step. Well, confident-looking. I think. I turn. "What are you waiting for?"

The walk is long, more than a mile, and when the bridge moves in the breeze, I grab the railing with clenched fingers. And Kip teases me. But the view of the Bay from the top is beautiful. The moon gleams, and the lights of houses reflect magic on the dark water.

"It's so pretty," I whisper. It's so quiet. So quiet I can hear Kip breathing lightly next to me. I could kiss him. So easily, just kiss him. Okay, it might not be that easy, but still.

He nudges me, and we jog down the decline of the bridge. At the end, breathing hard, we stop. To the left is the inlet to the creek, and beyond that is the fence for the base.

For a while, we walk along the edge of the fence, and with each step my nerves get more and more erratic. My heart pounds so loudly, I'm sure the entire Navy hears it, like they've already called in the helicopters.

Lydia's dad used to be in the Navy, and they drive over here to shop at the commissary. But I've never been on the base before, so I don't know what to expect. I know they have to show identification, so we can't just walk through the gate. Are there guards everywhere? Will they be waiting for us?

Behind the cover of loblolly pines, I see a small opening in the fence. Kip pushes through the gap and waves his hand for me to follow. His hair is so bright, I'm certain we'll be spotted immediately.

This is a test. I follow the rules. Passing through the fence will change that, and I debate the outcome in my head. My gut tells me it's a terrible decision, but I clench my fists and duck under the wire.

I expect some immediate reaction, but nothing happens. No alarm. No blinding lights. No military police.

"Okay," I say, whispering. "What are we doing here, other than breaking a million federal laws?"

"Shh, felon." He walks toward the water, phone away so we aren't spotted. The ships are huge steel mountains rising out of the black water.

"Are we allowed near these?"

He doesn't respond but keeps walking down different docks, like he's looking for something. After a few minutes, he stops and points in the dark. "Look right there, Murph!" Without lights, I have to strain to see. I make out a faint silhouette against the inky sky.

I gasp. A submarine.

I glance in Kip's direction and then back out at the water. Rising out of it, so it's only partially exposed, is a matte-black submarine with USS *New York* in white stenciled letters on the side.

"Kip!"

"I remembered a boater told me they're storing it here for a while before it's repaired and makes its way down to the submarine base in Georgia. Cool, huh?"

"Very." I take a few steps farther down the dock. "I know we saw pictures, but I didn't think it would be this size. It's as big as the whole island." Like a killer whale coming up for air, the sub's back is showing, its dull black sail like a fin.

I face Kip Dwyer as waves hit the dock. He thought of me. "It's amazing."

"I know you were upset about Ford Wallace. I wanted to cheer you up." Kip steps close to me, and my stomach flutters.

He thinks we can do this—build a sub. Maybe we can. Maybe I can read Wallace's book when I'm not volunteering at the library with Betty. Maybe I can even read it while I'm there, when the books are all put back on the shelves in the right order. And maybe when I get home, Kip and I can fix up the propane tank. I grin at him.

We don't need anyone's help.

Before I can thank him, lights and the sirens that come with them blare at the end of the dock.

12

Doors to a military police vehicle open and slam shut. Voices yell, "Don't move! Hands up!"

"Then how are we supposed to put our hands up?" Kip mumbles.

The next few moments are a blur. We are asked questions. Kip answers with jokes. And then we are in the back of a police car. This is it. The one time I break the rules, I'm going to be thrown in jail. Murphy's Law.

I'm praying and sweating and bouncing my knees so hard, Kip nudges me and whispers, "We didn't do anything wrong. Relax."

How could I possibly relax? The police take us to a small building a few minutes away from the docks. The two men in the front seat are quiet and don't look much older than teenagers. When we stop, they each get out of the car, then open the doors to lead us out. Strapped to their sides are the largest guns I've ever seen.

This is what I get for breaking rules. I'm not even in high school. Can't even drive. And I am going to prison. I don't want to think about what my dad will do, but the idea punches me in the stomach.

I talk to Joan and then to the queen. *Please, Mary, don't let them use those guns on us. Amen.* The more guardians watching over us, the better.

One of the sailors wraps his fingers around my arm, which makes me cringe, and walks me to the door of the brick building, his gun bumping against his hip. "Go get the lieutenant. Tell him we've got kids trespassing."

"Yes, sir." The one with Kip—the name tag on his chest says Smith—turns and leaves us in the front room of what must be the military police building. The jail. Maybe I'll spend the rest of my life here. Joan did. And my father is certainly familiar with the cold cinder blocks.

From what I can piece together, Smith comes back with someone more in charge, the lieutenant. He's older, tall and handsome like a movie star playing a military hero, with slick black hair and a trim mustache.

"Put them in there," he says. He points to a door. I gulp, imagining various forms of torture behind it.

They make us empty our pockets into a plastic bowl. Well, Kip's. I don't have pockets. I have nothing. Not even my Joan card. Kip and I walk into the room, and Smith shuts us in, leaving just the two of us. Kip sits in a metal chair.

"How should we plan our escape?" he asks. He leans back like he's in the science lab.

I glare at him and stand in the corner.

"What? They can't arrest us. We're minors. The worst thing they can do is call our parents."

I clasp my hands together. That's what I'm afraid of.

"Murph, sit down. It's not a big deal."

He says it like he gets taken in by military police all the time. I ease onto the chair but sit on the edge, my toes pointed, knees tight together. I don't lean back or get comfortable.

"It's a great first date, though," Kip says. He winks.

Only Kip Dwyer would consider this romantic. "You wish it was a date," I mumble.

"Ah, there she is!" He laughs out of pure joy. He is so frustrating. "Worth it, Murph. Totally worth it. We're gonna finish this sub as soon as we get out."

He should say if. *If* we get out.

The older man walks in and sits behind the metal table. He drops a folder on the silver top. I don't know how to act. He doesn't have a gun like the younger boys, but still.

"I'm Lieutenant Garcia."

"Lovely night, isn't it, sir?" Kip asks.

If I weren't terrified, I'd groan aloud. Instead, I turn and stare at him. This isn't Fen. He has to be serious.

Lieutenant Garcia pushes his chin down and regards Kip for a long time, the silence hovering over the three of us. I hold my breath. Garcia looks at me. "No identification? No reason to be wandering the base at oh two hundred hours?"

I think he means two in the morning.

"Kids live on base," Kip says. "You don't know we don't. You can't arrest people walking around their own houses."

"Were you at your house, son?" Garcia raises his eyebrow and leans over the table. "I wasn't under the impression you were in housing." He looks down at the papers that must include the information we gave to the sailors, like our names.

Before Kip can answer, I say, "No, sir."

"Last week a group of teenagers graffitied one of the hangars. Any idea who that might have been? Did you vandalize federal property?"

My eyes go wide. "No, sir. We were looking at the submarine." I don't know if that's illegal, but we didn't destroy anything.

"You expect me to believe that?"

"We were on a date, Lieutenant. I took her to see the submarine." The way Kip says it sounds sarcastic. Because Kip always sounds like he's joking around. It's the upturn of his nose or the gap in his teeth. I'm not sure which.

"You took your girlfriend to see a sub?" Garcia meets my eyes.

"I'm not his girlfriend," I mumble.

"That doesn't matter to me, miss."

"Yes, of course, sir." Embarrassed, I look down at my feet, and my hair spills around me. My outfit is ridiculous. I should have put on normal clothes, but then again, I didn't know I would end my night in jail. It seems like I put my shoes on five years ago.

"I'm very romantic, so yeah, I took my lady to see a sub."

I need him to stop talking. Or not be flippant. Or at least not say *my lady*.

"Son, you and your parents are about to be charged with a federal offense. I would shape up and tell the truth." The lieutenant's voice is sharp and commanding, a bark that may turn into a snap of jaws.

A federal offense. I don't even know what that means. I really need my Joan card. I press my fingers against the frayed edge of my nightgown, but it doesn't help.

And even though I can usually hold my sadness back, tears fill my eyes, then pour down my cheeks.

Next to me, Kip's voice softens. "It's my fault, sir. I knew she'd want to see the sub. It's the truth. We just did a project on them, and she wants to pilot one across the Bay. I thought she'd like to see the USS *New York*. Mary didn't do anything wrong."

Lieutenant Garcia stands up and clicks his pen. He leaves. He doesn't say where he's going or when he'll be back. He doesn't tell us if he's checking out our story or if he's sending the sailors to find evidence that we painted on the hangar. Nothing.

I wipe my face.

"I'm sorry, Murph. I didn't mean to make you cry. I shouldn't have brought you here. It was a bad idea. You forgive me?" Kip asks.

I stand up and jam my arms against my chest. Make myself as compact as possible. I don't know what I think.

"I haven't decided."

"Fair," he says.

We are quiet for a long time. Quiet and alone. I sit back down and prop my elbows on the table, watching the seconds tick by on the clock above the door.

I must fall asleep, because the next thing I know, the clock says four and the door is opening, Lieutenant Garcia barging through. I rub my eyes and stand. In the chair next to me, Kip is still asleep, his head back and mouth slack.

"Get up, Dwyer!" Garcia snaps.

Kip jumps up, dazed.

Garcia drops the same folder on the table. "Son, you're lucky your parents confirmed your story."

"I told you," Kip says, rubbing his eyes. "Romantic."

They called his parents. I ball my hands into fists. Did they call mine? I don't want to ask.

"This is what's going to happen. Seaman Smith is going to drive you home. You will show him the breech in the fence so this doesn't occur again. If I hear you were disrespectful or rude, you will be back here for the remainder of the night until I see fit. Do you understand me?"

"Yes, sir," we both say.

To me, Garcia says, "You need to pick better friends."

In the dark, Smith drives us to the hole in the fence and parks on the road. Kip curses under his breath while we walk through the grass.

A few hours ago, we walked through the same grass, but now we're accompanied by an armed guard. But Lieutenant

Garcia is wrong. I don't need to pick better friends. Kip might force me to move through the world louder than I want to, and without Kip, I wouldn't have gone to jail. But without Kip, I wouldn't be building a submersible either.

"Kip." I touch his elbow while Smith talks on the radio attached to his vest. "Thanks for showing me the sub."

He grins. "Told you it was a good first date."

"We could have been shot."

Back in the squad car, I smile out the window as we drive across the bridge back to our county. I know there are towering mountain ranges all over the world, but this has to be the tallest view. And the prettiest.

The car pulls up to the house on Bleecker Street, and I stop smiling. My father's truck, absent hours ago, is now parked in the driveway.

And he is waiting on the porch.

13

It's Saturday, so I sleep. I sleep the whole time, the whole day, buried under a blanket even though it's the end of May and hot on the Chesapeake. Like clockwork, my mother hands me two ibuprofen and a glass of water every six hours. We're a team when this happens. I take the medicine, drink the water, and hide back under the covers.

My mom calls Aunt Betty and tells her I can't volunteer. That I'm sick. Betty asks if I want to work at the library over the summer, with a real paycheck.

I can't think about it yet.

On Monday morning, I finally wake up. My side hurts, but groaning, I manage to get out of bed without Mom's help. I walk to the bathroom and refuse to look in the mirror right away.

After I wet my comb under the tap, I brush carefully, like I do every morning. But I can't. I stop. It hurts too much. My eye pulses, and every time I run the teeth through my hair, a pain surges down the left side of my body. I put the comb down on the edge of the sink.

I have avoided this moment for forty-eight hours, but I fix my eyes ahead. In complete contrast to my colorless face is a bruise. Brilliant, purple, and dark on my cheek. Warm tears slide down the mark and fall on the bathroom floor. I'm mad. It is a punishment for happiness.

Joan wouldn't let this happen.

Instead of putting my hair in braids, I run my fingers over my waves. If I keep my head down and hair forward, I might be able to hide it for the last week of school. I sigh. Only one more week, and then I'll be stuck on Bleecker Street until August.

In my room, I pull on my uniform and wish the fabric were soft. On my desk, next to Wallace's book, is the model sub Kip and I built. I touch the remote and imagine myself under the waves, thousands of miles away from Bournes.

My mom is waiting for me in the kitchen. "Don't you think school is a bad idea? You could stay home for a few days." Her eyes are still on the table, on the water stain in the wood.

I know why she doesn't want me to go to school. I've skipped it before, many times, but I don't want to today. "I can't. I have five tests this week. Finals." Science is first.

"I could call Sister Eu and ask her to drop them off. You could take them here."

Like I would be able to take them in the house where my father is smoke that bumps against the ceiling during a fire. I need to crawl on my belly just to get any air.

"I'm not doing that." If I don't have school, I have nothing. "I need to review with my teachers."

She points to my eye. "What will you say if anyone asks?" For my whole life, I've done what she's asked. I took a few days off and said I was sick. *I hurt myself. I fell.*

I hate it.

"What do you want me to say?" I cross my arms.

"He didn't mean to. He feels awful about it." She says what she always says, but I've never heard *him* speak those words. Never heard an apology leave *his* mouth.

"Sure he does." It hurts to roll my eyes.

"He had a hard day out on the water. They ran out of gas and needed someone to haul them in."

It is not a reason.

"And then you got out of a cop car with that Dwyer boy."

"This is not Kip's fault."

"You never got in trouble before him."

It's not Kip's fault, and it's not my fault. I push past her and stumble out the door.

My goal for the day is to pass by as seamlessly and silently as I usually do, gliding in and out of classes so the other kids can't remember if I was in school. But I forget that nothing changes at Our Lady Star of the Sea, and my hair—the braids I've worn every day since kindergarten—is different. I thought no one would notice.

At my locker, I get a visitor. Lydia. She hasn't talked to me since the gazebo. "I thought we had a new kid." Her voice is soft. "Your hair."

My back is still to her, my face buried in my locker. I have to tell her. If I don't, it will burst out of me. "My dad came home. He's been back since March. I should have told you then. You're right, I don't tell you anything, and I should."

"How's it going with him back?"

I turn around. It looks dramatic, I'm sure, because Lydia curses.

"Mary, you can stay with me. Just stay with me. Just live with us."

It's so easy to say that. Just move. But Lydia's family is perfect. She doesn't understand. She's never understood.

While she's staring, Kip bounds up. I face the chip in the navy blue of my locker, my hair a protective shield. I don't want him to see me. My broken, damaged pieces. My stomach burns. At least Lydia's been here before. I don't even know how to explain to him.

"My dad's kinda annoyed," Kip says, "but he knows it's not your fault. He turned red, but I can still work on the sub."

He laughs. His voice is light, and he leans his body against the row of lockers. I was able to keep it from him for two months. For two months, Kip Dwyer liked me, and now . . . well. He will see what I am. I am the devastation after a storm. Flattened. Wreckage. Branches strewn and splintered.

"Did you wear your hair like that for me, Murph? Are we working after school?"

"Maybe," I whisper. If he still likes me, when he sees.

"What are you two talking about?" Lydia asks. I catch a glimpse of her staring at Kip, one eyebrow raised.

"We're making a submarine," Kip says. "Even though we got arrested." He starts humming and singing the song, "We all live in a—"

"What?" Lydia puts an arm on my back, and I'm quiet. I wish I were louder. "Have some compassion, Kip."

He's quiet, like he's trying to figure out her words. "What's going on?" he asks.

I turn and drop my chin to my chest. Blink at my too-tight shoes, the toe scuffed and gray, raw and dull against the shiny black. I push my hair away from my face.

"Mary?" he whispers. "What happened?"

My throat aches. I clench my fists. I do not want to look at him. Or cry.

"Robert Murphy happened," Lydia says.

"Your dad did that?" Kip opens his mouth, shuts it, and rubs the back of his neck. I like when he does that. I like him, but he's not going to like me. I know it. His eyes are still on my face, which makes me want to break apart.

"He can't do that. He can't do that to you," he pleads. "Did you tell someone? The police? Sister Eu?"

"Please don't," I tell them both. "Please? I just want to take my finals, okay? And then it will be fine." My eyes are hot. *Please stop looking at me, Kip. Please.* I don't like when his face is somber. Grave.

"I hate him," he whispers.

The first bell rings, and Lydia takes my hand. "Come on, Mary. Let's go to the bathroom. I've got makeup in my bag." I feel Kip's eyes on us as Lydia leads me down the hall.

She steers me into the girls' bathroom and walks to the mirror with her makeup bag. She wipes her eyes off with a little sheet. On her lashes, she swipes mascara, puts it back, and rummages around until she pulls out a white tube. "Concealer," she says. "This is about Kip? And getting arrested? You'll have to tell me about that."

"I will."

Lydia studies my face, then squeezes the tube out on the back of her hand. She dips her finger in the makeup. When she taps lightly around my eye, I wince. "Sorry," she says. "This is darker than you are, but at least it's a skin color. Purple isn't supposed to be."

We haven't talked in so long, but it feels like no time has passed. I start to cry.

"I'm almost done," she says softly.

"It's not my cheek. I miss you. I'm sorry I didn't tell you."

She stops and screws the top back on. Her shoulders fall. "I missed you too. Do you want to stay with us for a few days?

I'm sure my parents won't care. I'll text my mom." Lydia pulls out her phone and waits for me to answer.

"Only if she doesn't call anyone. Please?"

Lydia purses her mouth and scratches her arm. "Okay." She sends a message, then shoves her phone away. She puts on her backpack and pulls on one of her twists in front of the mirror.

"Lydia? Thanks."

She hugs me lightly. "We've been best friends since we were babies." She squeezes my hand. "I'll see you seventh period. Good luck today."

I'm definitely going to need it.

I think I'm pretty inconspicuous, stealthy even. Mr. Fen stands over my table a little longer than usual, but when I snatch the review material out of his hand and fix my eyes on it, he shrugs and says, "New do, new Mary. Got it, kid," and moves on to the next pair.

The next five periods are the same, and I'm not even sure my French teacher realizes that it's me in the front row.

But Sister Eu is different. I should have known. The nun asks me to stay after religion class, and I silently curse. This, historically, has not gone well for me.

I lean against the desk and let my hair fall forward to cover my cheek.

"Mary," she says, watching me carefully, "I have a confession to make." I can feel her gaze even though my eyes are on the floor. I slide my hand in my pocket and hold the card tight.

"My confession is a little embarrassing."

"Okay, Sister." The longer she takes, the more uncomfortable I get. What could she possibly confess, and why to me? It doesn't make any sense.

"Yes, and it's silly. I am, after all, a grown woman. It is perfectly reasonable for me to want to go there."

Aunt Betty always wants to talk about the nuns. She finds them fascinating. She says they aren't feminists, but I disagree. Other than Jesus, they aren't dependent on any man. Just like Betty's always talking about.

I need to talk to her about the summer. I need that job. I need money for the sub.

"What is it?" I glance up briefly. Sister Eu looks uncomfortable, which I find mesmerizing. How can I see that when she is covered up by a whole habit?

"I'm sorry. You must be curious, Mary. This is so much easier in front of Father Mike."

She waits and smooths out her habit. "Sometimes I go to the Tavern."

"The Tavern?" I'm not sure how she wants me to react. Sister Eu gave me the Joan card. Sister Eu bought me supplies when I got my period for the first time, in September. A drinking Sister Eu doesn't fit the ink smudge of dress in front of me. I don't like it.

"Yes."

The seconds between words are hours, and my head bounces from one idea to another. The silence makes me squirm. "Okay." I'm not sure why adults always expect kids to know what they're talking about, like we're mind readers. I wiggle my leg, sweating in my heavy skirt.

"I was there yesterday, and I heard your father talking about Kip. And I held that in my brain until today." She taps her temple. "And now I see your . . ." She waits. "Hair." The word hangs in the air, waiting for me to catch it.

My mother's words hang there too, and I'm afraid the two will collide.

"Is that all, Sister?" I stand up abruptly, and my side aches. I need more medicine.

As soon as she says, "Yes," I turn and head toward the door.

"Mary, I just . . ." The nun sounds like she's trying to find words. "If you need anything, or need to tell me something, please do, child."

"Thank you, Sister." I briefly look back, but when my feet cross the doorway, I bolt.

∿∿∿∿∿∿∿∿∿∿∿∿∿∿∿∿∿∿∿∿∿∿∿∿∿

I make it to math class on time and sink into my seat in the back, the same seat I've had the whole year. Lydia's up front, so she's in my class but not really, because Mr. Wisniewski hasn't moved us all year and we don't work in groups.

Usually, I don't mind because it's quiet, and I can turn off my brain. But today, I want to think about math. I don't want to think about Sister Eu and her confession.

Lydia turns around and mimes that she is going to write me a note. She hasn't done that since she got a phone for her birthday in October. She writes something down, rips the paper out, and hands it to a boy behind her.

The note travels back like a piece of driftwood, up and down the wave of hands. I glimpse at Mr. Wisniewski, his back to me, his hand a flurry at the board. He won't care. I suspect a lot of teachers pretend they don't see notes or phones.

When it gets to me, I unfold the paper.

You need to get a phone! How is today going? Anyone notice? Have you talked to Kip?

Those are easy. *I know! Okay. Maybe Sister Eu. No.* Kip and I might never talk again. And never hold hands again. Never go on any adventures again. I try not to think about it or the nun. I refuse to. I don't even want to tell Lydia about it, but that's the thing about best friends. They make you talk.

At the end of class, Lydia drags me down the hall to our lockers.

"You're hurting me."

"No, I'm not. Why do you think Sister Eu knows?"

"My dad, weirdly enough. I'll tell you more in a second." I want to be outside first.

"Your dad?" It looks like her head might explode. She scrambles to get her backpack filled and waits impatiently for me. When I finish packing up, we rush through the halls.

"Let's go, Murphy!" Outside the church, she skips steps ahead of me. I stop and smile. Maybe things are back to normal with Lydia. But then I feel guilty and uncomfortable. I wish my dad hitting me wasn't my normal.

I can't let it be. From the top of the steps, I say, a little too loud, "I'm going to build a sub, Lydia."

She turns around and smiles up at me. "I love it!"

"I'm going to build it, but I need help. I can't do it by myself." Or just with Kip, if he even wants to help anymore. I need Ford Wallace. I follow my friend down the steps of Our Lady. "I have to go to the Scientists' Retreat, but I'll meet you at your house after."

∿∿∿∿∿∿∿∿∿∿∿∿∿∿∿∿∿∿∿∿∿∿∿∿∿

I take the long way along the shore, my heart a wobbly mess as I stand in front of cottage number twelve. Before I even knock, behind me, I hear "I didn't think I would see you again, my dear."

Ford Wallace walks toward me from the driveway smiling, but when he sees my face, he stops. "Are you okay?"

"No." I shake my head slowly because it aches, and my hair swirls around me, a black cloud. "I am not okay." It feels good to say those words. I've never said them. *I'm fine. I'm fine*, I usually say. But I'm not fine.

I plant my feet and say, "If you don't help me, I will die."

"Now, darling, that can't possibly be true."

"I think it's the truest sentence I've ever said."

Ford Wallace rubs the scruff on his jaw. "You certainly are earnest."

"Please help me." My words vibrate through me. They start down in the soles of my feet and race through my body.

Wallace sighs, his shoulders falling while he breathes out. "You have until August first. That's when I leave for Japan."

My legs are weak. I keep nodding until he walks into the cottage. *He's going to help me.* I press my fingers to my smile. I have seven weeks to build a sub.

15

I spend the night at Lydia's. I don't call the Murphy house.
I don't need to. My dad disappears for a few days when this
happens, and my mom will know I'm with Lydia. And Lydia
and I talk, really talk, for the first time in months over our
books and packets and notes. In her pink bedroom full of
posters of bands and rappers I've never heard of, the two of
us sit on her bed. I tell her the story about the base, and her
jaw drops each time I mention guns.

"Why do you want to build a sub?" she asks, hopping off
the bed. "Like for me and my animations, I like making a new
world. It's socially acceptable pretend, but it's okay because
it's creative and I get to share it."

I look around her room. Clothes and projects litter the
floor, and one whole wall is covered in Lydia's artwork. In

the corner is her computer and video equipment, humming and blinking above her work in progress.

She walks over to the new set. "I should finish this one by the end of the summer. It's a princess story." She holds up a clay dragon. "But there's a twist. The princess saves herself. No need for a knight." Lydia puts the small molded sword in my hand.

"I want to be my own knight," I answer. "That's why."

~~~~~~

In the morning, Lydia borrows her mom's makeup and helps me again. A blue stain on my face, the bruise refuses to be completely covered. It will get uglier before it heals, turning all shades before it disappears. Lydia's mom drives us to school, where I have three finals, science my first and toughest.

When I walk into class, I say hi to Fen and shake my head at his rumpled shirt. If I had money, I'd get him an iron for an end-of-the-year present. But any money I earn from the library will go to the sub.

After morning prayer, Mr. Fen says, "Are you ready to fail this test?"

Everyone groans, but Fen laughs. "You think I'm joking, but I'm not."

More groans fill the lab. Kathleen hands me the thick packet of questions, and I write my name on the front page.

Mr. Fen reads the official directions, and I exhale. The room is quiet, and I open to the first question. I pat my pocket with Joan's card. I can do this.

A few minutes later, I hear the classroom door open. Sister Eu silently moves through the room. My heart drops when she walks to Fen's desk and whispers. I clench my pencil. He looks at me—*Oh Lord*—and motions for me to come up. I look around the room and see everyone's eyes on me, including Kip's.

My gaze at the ceiling, I walk across the classroom. Sister Eu points to the door, and I say, "But I have a final, Sister." It might be rude, but there's no way it's a good thing I'm being pulled out of this test. And as awful as Fen makes it sound, I'm sure I'll pass.

I am less sure about Sister Eu.

She ushers me out of the room silently.

As soon as she shuts Fen's door, she turns to me and says, "There's someone who needs to speak with you in my office, Mary."

"Who is it, Sister?"

She doesn't say anything, only walks briskly in the direction of the main office, her habit swishing at her feet. I am a crab about to hit the steam pot. Pounded with a mallet. Picked apart. I hesitate.

"This way, Mary."

I mutter under my breath and follow. The school office is freezing, the air-conditioning blasting, and Mrs. Rivers, the school secretary, is on the phone with a parent. It sounds like an angry one, because she keeps trying to finish a sentence but can't.

Sister Eu's door is closed. I look at the nun's kind face.

"Go in, please," she says. "I will be right here if you need me." She sits in one of the blue chairs lining the wall.

Joan sat in front of rows of men, waiting for the inquisitors to tell her if she had broken any laws. "You are putting yourselves in great peril," she warned them. They were terrified. I square my shoulders.

I don't have an option, so I open the door and step in.

Sitting in Sister Eu's chair is a man I've seen before, only, time has aged him in the last few years. Gray hairs have cropped up around the temples and a slightly bigger stomach pushes against his shirt. The same dark brown skin and soft eyes though.

"Good morning, Mary."

"Mr. Harris."

"How are you? It's been a while." He pages through what I assume is the Mary Murphy case file. "Three years?" He smiles up at me. "That's a good sign." He shifts in his chair. Mr. Harris is my social worker. He carries a red nylon bag filled with other files.

I don't speak. It's always best not to speak in front of social workers. If you're not careful, they will send you to foster care. To some family that might be even worse than yours. To a new school where you know no one.

Three years ago, the school reported the marks around my wrist, and I told Mr. Harris I was allergic to the metal in my bracelet.

I cross my arms and sit.

"I don't come down to the island very much. Y'all don't have much to say." He laughs a little. "Hard to get a word out of you."

I lean forward so my hair covers my face more.

"Do you know why I'm here, Mary?"

"No." *Obviously, I do.*

"What happened Friday night?"

I shrug. "Nothing that I can remember."

"Hmm," he says. "That's odd. Must have been a different thirteen-year-old Mary Murphy taken into custody by base police. I'll have to follow up with Lieutenant Garcia." He writes something down in his notes.

"Okay, yes." I roll my eyes. I know I'm acting like a brat, but I have a huge test that no one seems to care about.

"Why don't you tell me what happened," he says gently. Mr. Harris has eyes that make you want to tell him the truth. I scowl at them.

I tell him a lot of it. Most of it. Some of it. And he nods his head.

"How did Mom and Dad react?" He stops writing and looks me straight in the eye. I squirm.

"They don't know," I lie. I lift my chin to stop myself from crying. "So I would appreciate it if you wouldn't tell them." My tears are real, even if my words are not.

"You know I have to follow up with them."

"Yes." Social workers always check to see if your stories match. I'm sure my mother will pretend like she didn't know.

"And how did you hurt your eye?" He doesn't look at me, only the desk with his papers.

"What?" I whisper.

"Your eye, Mary."

He says it like he already knows. Someone told him. Who? Sister Eu? Betty? I haven't even seen her. Kip? Lydia's family?

I squeeze my knees together. Someone told on me. The mutiny stings as much as my bruise. "I fell."

Mr. Harris writes instead of talking, then looks up. "I hear that one a lot. Lots of clumsy people in the county." His voice drops. "Your dad's on probation for assault? Just released from prison?"

"Yes, but not for assaulting me." I am a rockfish refusing to bite, and frustration is leaking off the waterman.

"Mary, I want you to know that you're in a position to help yourself. You can tell me anything, and I can help. That's my job."

"Right." What if the truth did come out? What if it unraveled like a rope?

"I'm serious. I'm here for you." He packs up his nylon bag and pulls a card out of his wallet, the edges curved. He hands it to me.

My throat aches. My brain hurts. My eyes commit treason. "Are we done, Mr. Harris? I'm missing my final."

"One last thing, Mary. I know you're not telling me everything. And you know I can't do anything unless you do. But if you don't want to talk to me, I suggest talking to someone, an adult you can trust."

I don't wait for a pass from Mrs. Rivers, and I don't stop when Sister Eu calls my name. Instead, I hurry, trying not to sprint like a weirdo down the hallway back to class. I need to take that test.

I burst back into the room, and everyone looks up from their exams. My noise is much louder than the classroom noise, and I panic, stepping back into the hall.

I slump against the wall, my feet tucked neatly underneath me. When the doorknob turns, I lift my head. Mr. Fen is standing over me, his shoes inches from me.

His body halfway in the door, Mr. Fen scolds the other students. "What are you looking at? You have a test to take. I swear, if you even think about cheating, I will give you a zero." His face is growly. "Not that any of you think anyway."

Then he crouches down, the door open a crack. "You okay?"

"I'm fine." Kip would know what *fine* means, but I'm not sure he even likes me anymore.

"Well, from that entrance, I'm thinking perhaps you're not."

"Mr. Fen, sir, I *am* fine," I insist. I stand, and now it's weird again because I'm standing and he's kneeling.

"Because if you want to take the test later, I understand."

Was it him? Did Mr. Fen tell on me? Doesn't he know this just makes everything worse? "I want to take the test now."

"Are you sure?"

"Mr. Fen." My voice is too loud. "I appreciate your concern, but yes, I would like to be normal and take my test with the rest of the class. Stop feeling sorry for me." I brush past him, and that feels weird too. I keep doing all this weird stuff, when all I want to do is take my test like a regular eighth grader.

I sit back down next to Kathleen, rearrange my pencils, and try to ease the pounding in my chest. Three questions in, I peek at Fen. My cheeks fall. He was being nice.

With the last thirty minutes of class, I finish the test with no time to worry about the visit from Mr. Harris.

16

I see Kip in my classes, but we don't sit close enough to talk. And after school, I can't find him, so I head to the marina before my meeting with Ford Wallace. I would rather be doing anything else. Does Kip want to help still? Does he still like me? What does he think of me now that he knows?

I don't know if I want the answers to any of those.

Mrs. Dwyer smiles when I walk in the shop and tells me Kip's out on gas duty while Monica yanks on her arm. I brace myself as I walk out toward Back Creek and the dock. I'm going to tell him about Ford Wallace. I'm going to tell him and let him decide what he wants to do. I squeeze my fingers into fists.

This time, he is alone at the gas pump, sitting on an overturned bucket that's probably used for chum. I'm so quiet, he doesn't see me until I'm standing right in front of him. When he does, he shoots up. He's a lot taller than I am, and I swear he's grown in the last two months. Inches. Feet. A few docks down, a boat motor starts, and Kip looks behind him.

"Hi," I say.

"Hey, Mary."

I shake my head. Mary doesn't sound right. It's the Kip Dwyer kiss of death. "I'm going to the retreat right now. Ford Wallace said he'd help me." I try to make my voice normal.

"Are you sure you . . ." Kip keeps looking at my eye. And at my cheek. And out at the water so he doesn't have to look at my eye or cheek. It's awful. It's embarrassing. I am very sick of my eyes burning and people feeling sorry for me. Pity is the worst. I would gladly replace it with almost anything.

I cross my arms. "Yes, I am going to build this sub, and you can help me or not."

Kip puts his hand on the back of his neck where the sun has made it red. "If I didn't bring you across the bridge. If I didn't get us in trouble, he wouldn't have . . . I'm sorry. I'm really, really sorry."

"It is not because of you."

"But what if he . . . ?" Kip frowns, which I've never seen, I don't think. Not a real frown. It must be because he doesn't like me. He doesn't. That's why he doesn't want to help.

"You don't like me anymore, I get it," I say. "I understand." But I don't want it to be true. I ball my hands even tighter and jam them in my pockets.

"What?" he asks. "Murphy, that's the most . . . Are you serious? I'm pretty sure I've made my affection very clear." He laughs, which is a nice sound to hear, even if he is laughing at me. "Fen said too clear! I know I shouldn't be taking advice from him, but my dad, he's a little too good with the ladies."

I don't laugh along with him, so his freckles get serious again.

"I feel like it's my fault." Kip watches me very carefully while he talks. "I don't want him to hurt you again."

Before, I wanted to build the sub for selfish reasons. To spend time with Kip. To build something with my hands like we built the remote-controlled version. To escape, at least in stolen moments. For minutes, for hours, I could forget about my dad. I could forget about the damage he's caused.

But now I want those minutes to extend. To expand like a bubble. To turn into something else.

I stick out my chin and look up at Kip. "What's the worst he could do?"

"I don't know," Kip says. His face isn't as carefree as usual. It's too serious. "But if you're in, I'm in."

Dedicated to fighting for France's freedom, Joan sought out a French captain who knew the dauphin, Charles. Once he'd decided Joan wasn't a witch, the captain gave her a sword, an expensive horse, and four soldiers to guard her as she traveled to the dauphin. For protection on the dangerous roads, she cut her hair short and dressed like the male soldiers. At night, she slept on the ground in armor.

When she met Charles, she curtsied and whispered a secret God had told her. A secret no one but the dauphin knew.

The dauphin accepted her pledge to help him be crowned.

Destiny was coming true.

Joan trained alongside the soldiers. The voices told her she would find a sword, lost for hundreds of years, at Saint Catherine's tomb. At her saint's place of rest, the sword appeared, five crosses engraved in its metal.

And then she was ready for battle.

Her tale spread across France. How she was gifted and fast. Able to ride a horse and fight. Hundreds of men came to fight for her. And then thousands.

Joan wore a suit of gleaming armor. Into battle, she carried a banner, a beautiful painting of Jesus and Mary and the fleur-de-lis.

The saints told her she would not last the year, so she was impatient for victory. Joan ignored the advice of the military leaders and rallied the troops to victories in Orleans first, and then along the Loire River.

And then it was time. Charles was ready to be crowned. At his coronation, Joan stood by his side as he was anointed.

She had done it. She had gotten France their king.

17

My side hurts less, and I ride my bike to the Cliffs without Kip. He has to work until dark. When Wallace opens the door, he says, "Hi, dear" with a drawl and a smile. I like the nice Ford Wallace.

He ushers me in and points to the couch.

"Can I get you anything to eat or drink?" he asks, busying himself in the kitchen. It's the only uncluttered spot in the house. When I shake my head, he says, "I'm just going to get myself some coffee. I have a bit of a problem with caffeine. Drink too much of it." He hurries over with his coffee, the syrupy smell following him, and moves a pile of books off a chair.

"Now, what is the goal? Where is your sub going to take you?"

Away. "Across the Bay."

Ford rummages around in a pile in the corner and spreads out a contour map of the water on the coffee table. My dad has the same map; the black lines show the depth of the Bay.

"If you leave from the marina, it'll be about seven miles. That's conceivable as far as oxygen and the supplies we can get." He rubs his knuckle along the hair on his jaw. "You read my book?"

I nod. A chunk of it. Some of Kip's and my earlier ideas were wrong, and I'm glad I didn't trust us on our own.

"Building a submersible today is a lot like when I wrote the book in 1976, only technology is better now. But the science is the same." He pats my hand. "We're going to get creative. Mix a little old with the new to save money."

I tell him about the propane tank at Dwyer's Marina, and he squeals.

"We'll draft out a plan on a program today. How much do you know about CAD?"

Nothing. "What's CAD?"

"We are going to make a 3-D design of your submersible on my computer."

We stack the papers on his desk and move away the books, then he opens a blank white project on his screen and makes me sit. For three hours, and with his help, I figure out how to build a model of the submersible.

I start with the hull, the sub's body. If I were rich, or working for a lab or STEM program, we could make it out of plastic, designing and building the body from scratch. But like Ford Wallace said, we are mixing old and new.

I look up the measurements of the kind of propane tank they have at the marina—six feet long and two and a half feet high—and plug them into the software. I add another five inches to the top of the sub, right in the middle. A bubble that will become the hatch. A 3-D image of my sub appears, and I hide a smile behind my hand.

"We need to include the hatch," I tell Ford, who wants me to call him by his first name. "And a porthole." I count the parts out on my fingers. "Oh, a ballast, a battery, lights, and a motor." All things I've talked about with Kip.

How are we going to power it? In the book, in the section titled "Power Distribution," I read my options. When we weigh them out, we settle on marine batteries. I can get them at Dwyer's. I just need to save up some money.

When I leave the Scientists' Retreat, I ride my bike home, the sun shining, blaring, trumpeting above me. My face is probably doing the same.

18

Two days later is my last day of school. I tell Mr. Fen good-bye and thank him for the project. I still haven't told him about the real sub that I'm working on with Ford. But that feels like a wonderful secret to keep mostly to myself. When it's real, I'll tell. Well, I'll tell some people. Trustworthy people.

Mr. Dwyer drives the propane tank up to Ford's cottage that afternoon, and Kip and Ford and I work on the computer, making alterations to our design.

Friday, the first morning of break, I leave Lydia's and hope that everything has blown over at home. I get ready early for the library, and he's already gone out on the water. Betty drives down to Bournes and picks me up in her hybrid to take me to North Beach in the middle of the county. I start my first job. My first real job that pays actual money.

My hair down, I sit next to her. I like her car. I like the

leather seats and the long drive. The smell of the Bay. The old tobacco barns, the paint stripped off. NPR on the radio. She never complains about the drive either.

But today she doesn't start the car like usual. Instead, she says, "Let me see you."

I move really fast to face her, then cover myself.

"I told you we were going to be honest with each other," she says. "I don't operate any other way."

I turn my head but don't meet her eyes.

"Did he do that?"

I don't say anything. I like Betty, I really do. I just don't know her all that well yet.

"Is he here?"

I shake my head.

She fixes her glasses and backs out of the driveway.

For the rest of the day, she teaches me what is expected of an assistant at the library. I will work in the computer lab. Technically, I'm not old enough for working papers, so Betty will pay me in cash until my birthday in a few weeks. Once I turn fourteen, I will get a real paycheck.

Over the shelves of books, she watches me with her eyebrows pushed down. A mirror to mine when I'm distressed. But she says nothing about my face. It makes me squirm. Worse than when I'm with Sister Eu. I wait the entire time for the other shoe to drop.

When her hours are done, Betty drives me back down. The pickup truck with the dented bumper is not parked at my house when I go to open the car door.

"Oh no," she says. "We're going to make another stop."

I put my hands in my lap. *Where?* She turns down Bleecker Street, and at the roundabout, she takes the first turn, down toward the bars on the end of the island. I put my hand against my jean pocket, where Joan lays hidden.

At the Tavern, Betty stops. Two men are walking in the door, men I've seen before. *Why are we at the Tavern?* I squint while she gets out and shakes her hair back. My father's truck is parked at the end.

"You stay right here," she says. "I'll be back in a minute."

"Yes, ma'am."

I fixate on the black door of my dad's favorite place. She comes out five minutes later, her face red. "If he ever does that again, you call me. You call me or the police. Or you run to a neighbor's house and call me." She buckles her seat belt, her fingers shaking. "I'm buying you a phone. Okay?"

"Okay," I say. The shoe drops. But she doesn't mention a social worker.

In the morning, she hands me a phone, and I tuck it in my backpack. I've never had one before.

At the library, I work in the adult computer lab. Mostly I help old people use Google and close browsers. I print off recipes and pictures of their grandchildren for them. Only a few people come in a day. The kid computer lab, on the other hand, is a bunch of frenzied fish going after bait. Chaos. But Betty's in charge of that.

We eat in the staff room together at lunch. Betty brings rice and beans and roasted vegetables from her garden. She packs a nut butter sandwich and pretzels for me with two glass bottles of water, but she sneaks purple soda from the vending machine every day and says, "Just this once."

In the afternoons, when I'm alone in the computer lab, I watch videos online and take notes. I could attach two wheels from a jogging stroller to the sub to launch it into the water. They don't weigh a lot and won't be in the way while I'm piloting. Or we could use a trailer for a boat or a Jet Ski to launch. I write down options to share with Ford and Kip.

I watch a researching team find new organisms never discovered before on the floor of waterways. And teenagers constructing submersibles and tanks.

I ask Betty for a notebook, and when she hands me one, I bring it into the lab and write "Ford Project" in neat letters on the blue cardboard cover. I draw waves underneath the letters and smile.

But it's not like Kathleen drawing unicorns. I'm really going to pilot a sub.

19

At the library and home, I finish Ford's book. The section on water accidents explains why Ford wanted me to have a lawyer. One small wave can flood a sub when it's exposed to the surface. Lots of people have died that way. And all the chemicals reacting in such a small area can cause fires and explosions.

Oxygen levels are another worry. Every thirty minutes, an alarm will go off, reminding me to open the oxygen valve. Too much, and I explode. Too little, and I choke. I pull my hair tight against my scalp at the nape and try to ignore the idea that I might not survive the trip.

The propane tank sits in Ford's driveway, the paint peeling off, a long white pill ready to transform. When it's quiet at the library, I daydream about the voyage. I'll be undetectable under the waves.

Two weeks into summer break, we work on the welding. Ford's neighbor, Mr. Jack, will do it for free. He just wants me and Kip to bring him shark teeth when we find them. He sells them along Route 4. That's easy. Kip brought him six yesterday.

"Go get Mr. Jack if you're ready," Ford shouts from the kitchen.

At cottage number ten, I knock. Mr. Jack, an old man with big gray hair and light brown skin, answers. He's wearing coveralls, even though it's a million degrees out, that protect his arms and legs. Tiny glasses sit on his nose.

"You'll need this so you don't get harmed." He hands me the large metal helmet in his hand. I put the heavy mask on, the inside hot. I must look like a villain in a horror movie.

Mr. Jack has a similar helmet in his hand. "You don't need it yet," he says. "We need to do something more important first."

I take the helmet off. "What?"

"You need to wash the tank, every square inch, so it doesn't have any impurities on the surface of the metal. And we need to scrape off the old paint." Mr. Jack is direct, which I appreciate, but I don't want to wash the metal. I thought we would be doing something fun, like cutting through the sub.

"Don't give me that look, girl. If we don't wash it, you could find yourself at the mercy of the Bay. Get a bucket, soap, and a sponge."

"Okay." I try not to sound grumpy. I run into Ford's cottage and get everything we need from the kitchen.

"What does he want you to do?" Ford asks, a coffee mug in his hand.

"Wash the tank. That doesn't sound very STEM to me," I complain.

"Trust me, it is. Cleanliness is next to . . . science-ness?" Ford laughs. "Just do it. He's going to spend hours doing this for you, Miss Mary. For free. You can wash the vessel." He shoos me back outside.

I wash the propane tank, my muscles aching under the sun. And then Mr. Jack makes me wash it again. The third time is apparently sufficient, because he finally lets me stop.

"Now I can get to work." He works slowly, which I know is part of the process, and I stand there, in my heavy helmet, handing the man supplies. Sparks fly as he cuts away a hole for the hatch.

I stand there for hours, sweating, my hair stuck to my face. When Mr. Jack is done for the day, I thank him and give him back the protective gear. We have more work to do tomorrow. Welding is a lot slower than I thought. I tell Ford good-bye and ride my bike to Lydia's.

One step closer to a voyage.

20

"Can't we just watch the fireworks from your porch like we usually do?" I ask, grabbing a soda out of Lydia's fridge.

"No, please?" Lydia whispers. "My parents never let me hang out with Omar unless it's a group." She salutes me as she talks. Her dad, the former military man, is strict. Well, not really strict, but Lydia thinks he is. "We're going."

I groan, and she flicks me in the shoulder. "But are you going to kiss Omar all night?" I ask. "Then I should definitely stay here."

Lydia smiles. "Oh, like you don't want to kiss Kip."

I'm probably doing the eyebrow thing. I don't know what I think about kissing. I've never done it before. I bite the inside of my cheek while we walk down to the beach for the fireworks. The third weekend of June is the Blessing of the Fleet. Father Mike says a prayer, the mayor smashes a bottle of champagne on a bow, and the whole island celebrates the boats.

We walk past crowds of people and find Omar with a bunch of Our Lady kids. Near the rock that juts out, separating the beach from the town, a ninth grader flattens a blanket, and Lydia and Omar sit. I smile at Omar putting his arm around her.

And panic a little too.

To relax, I look out at the water and think about silica gel, like the little packets that come in a shoebox. The gel helps control humidity, and in the sub, it will allow me to read the units on the controls.

The sun starts to set. It blazes fiercely over the Bay, desperately trying to stay in the sky. I take off my sandals and walk toward the water. Little girls splash off to our right, but no one is ahead. I wade. That's all I do. I really am a terrible swimmer.

Based on what Ford said, a strong swimmer could swim across the Bay in about the same time as the sub, two to three hours. I laugh out loud. I figure that engineering my own submersible is ultimately easier than learning how to swim.

"Are you telling jokes over there?" I hear behind me. "To who? Yourself?"

I turn around. "Hi."

As Kip walks closer, I watch his mouth. "Whatever the joke is, it can't possibly be as funny as I am."

"I'm funnier than you are."

"According to who, Murph?" Kip takes another step closer, his hair bright. He's really close to me now, our feet almost touching in the water. I pray there are no jellyfish. He grabs a lock of my hair, and I hold my breath. We seem alone, a lot more alone than when we actually are.

"Your hair's pretty," he says quietly. I'm still staring at his mouth. It's nice.

"Yours too," I say, exhaling. I don't know what I'm doing. My heart pounds in my ears.

Kip grins. The gap in his teeth shows. I like that gap. Still holding a strand of my hair, he leans close to my face.

Oh Lord. I think we're going to kiss. I don't know if I want to, if I'm ready. What if I mess it up? What if it's great? What if . . . so many possibilities. I take a step back. "I've never kissed anybody. Have you?"

"No." His voice is soft. "Unless you count when Kathleen tackled me on the playground in second grade and kissed my eyeball." He smiles, his eyes bright. "I have that effect on women." Only Kip would make a joke. I smile even though he's ridiculous.

"I don't think I'm ready," I say.

"Okay," he says. He shrugs in his floppy way, and I'm relieved.

Boom! A loud crack fills the sky. Kip's face lights up, and someone behind us whoops. The fireworks. Over on the blanket, the Our Lady kids have gathered. Omar gets up and runs over to us, grabbing Kip by the shoulders. He pulls him over to the blanket, and I follow.

We sit next to each other as magic fills the sky. Bright golds. Fizzing reds. Silver of fish scales. Happiness hums through me while Kip bumps my shoulder with his. "Glad I get to see you this summer, Mary Murphy. Never usually do."

"Me too."

At the end of the night, we all walk back together and drop off Omar first. Kip walks with me and Lydia to her house, the three of us weaving in and out of the crowds. People walk by singing loudly. When we get to Lydia's house, she and I run up the porch and leave Kip at the bottom of the steps.

But I don't want to leave him.

Feeling brave, I turn around and run back down. I grab him around the neck and hug him. His body is warm against mine, his T-shirt lightly touching my arm. He puts his hands on my waist. My cheek against his, I say, "I like you."

I pull away quickly and wave, walking into the house with Lydia, even though I'd rather stay outside, hugging for hours and hours.

We get ready for bed in Lydia's room, and I take my spot on the bed close to the wall. The air-conditioning blows against my face. I put my hand on my belly button and feel dizzy. I bet Joan never got to hug a boy in the dark.

"You like Kip Dwyer," Lydia says.

"I know."

"Like a lot."

"I know."

Lydia turns over and laughs, her face touching my pillow. "Remember when he hid those Halloween decorations in Miss Porter's ceiling?"

"Ugh, yes. He's so . . ." The ceiling kept cackling, and our fifth-grade teacher couldn't figure out why.

"He's liked you a long time."

I fall asleep smiling.

The next afternoon, under heavy gray clouds thickening the sky, I go to Ford's and see the cuts for the porthole and the hatch. I sprint over to Mr. Jack's cottage and knock, impatient. He comes to the door grumbling, which I hear even before he opens the door.

"Can we install them today?" I ask.

"I guess," he says. "Let me get all the tools. You're helping this time. My wrist is acting up. Think it's this weather." He rotates his hand and grimaces.

"Yes, sir."

"Stop standing around gawking, girl. Go get the hatch and the porthole."

I sigh and run over to Ford's for the pieces we got at the marine supply store up near the library. They're used. I wonder what their stories are. What they were used for, whose boat, whose life, and how they made their way to mine.

For the rest of the afternoon, I do what he tells me. He yells at me at least five times, calls me "little girl," but he can't see me roll my eyes with the helmet on. The porthole doesn't fit at first, so I have to use a tool that grinds down the metal. My arms are sore.

And then it looks like a real sub. When we pack up for the day, I thank him for teaching me. I crawl inside and look out through the porthole, a window to the water. Soon, I'll be underwater in this contraption, all by myself in the Bay. I gulp. I'm gonna need all the luck I can get. All the nuns at school to pray for me too, hands clasped, words in unison, until I land on the far shore.

~v~v~v~v~v~v~v~v~v~v~v~v~v~v~v~v~v~v

Three weeks into summer break, Betty hands me my first-ever income. She takes me to the bank after work, where we set up a savings account. Most of the money will go toward the sub, but I haven't told Betty about what I'm building just yet. Ford and I have planned out a budget, and a used motor is next on the list.

She takes me out to eat to celebrate my first paycheck, and her wife, Alex, joins us. She wears silver bracelets that sound like music when they clang together. She smiles kindly when Betty rants about a man at the library who refused to pay an overdue fine for a book he swore he had never taken out. I like them both. They feel steady.

When I'm not at the library, I'm at Ford's. And if I'm not at Ford's, I'm at the library. I love it. I haven't escaped to the Cliffs in a long time.

On Thursday during lunch, the phone Betty gave me rings in my backpack. She sips her grape soda and raises her eyebrows at me. "Are you going to answer that?"

I gave Ford my phone number. And Lydia. But I never asked Betty if that was okay. "Yes, ma'am," I say, but I don't move. I don't know if she's mad at me. I should have silenced it like I do at home. My dad would not like that Betty gave me a phone. He would say it was charity. My dad hates charity.

"It's okay to use your phone, Mary."

Ford is on the other end. He's using his sweet, happy voice, which worries me. "Miss Mary! How are you? Are you at the library?" It sounds windy. Like he's driving with windows down or walking outside.

"Yes." I frown. Why is Ford calling me?

"I met someone today down at the marina. I bought a charger from Kip's little sister. She is delightful, by the way. All those freckles on the Dwyers." A horn honks. "I'm headed to Annapolis for the night. I've got some friends in town. You can keep working at the cottage if you want. Ask Mr. Jack to let you in. I'll see you tomorrow afternoon just like we planned."

That's why he called me? To tell me about the Dwyers and say he was going out of town?

"I met your father!" Ford says. "Mr. Dwyer introduced me."

My stomach drops. "What?" I whisper. What did Ford tell him? What does my dad know?

Ford answers, but I can barely hear him. He's talking too fast. He's yelling over the wind, and I can't focus. I never told Ford about my father. Never told him that my father doesn't know about the sub. That he *can't* know about the sub.

Then Ford tells me to bring Mr. Jack a bread he made and says good-bye, and I hang up. Panic fills me. What will my father do if he found out that I'm hiding the sub from him? That I'm working with Ford? Did Ford mention Kip?

I squeeze my eyes shut and sigh. This can't be good.

When I look, Betty slides her glasses up her nose and doesn't ask me anything. I clear my throat. Better come out with it.

"I'm making something." I sigh. "I'm building a submarine."

"You're what? Where?" Betty leans over the table. "How?"

"I'm building a submersible, technically. With my friend Kip and a scientist who lives near the Cliffs."

"Why do you sound embarrassed? You say it like you were communicating with aliens. This is exciting." My aunt grins, folding her hands on the table.

For the rest of lunch, I tell Betty all about the sub, but with the heavy feeling in my chest that something is wrong.

After a successful campaign and crowning of Charles, Joan parted ways with the king, though the war wasn't over. She disagreed with his advisers about how to completely free France from English rule. On her way to a reception in her honor, trapped outside the walls of a safe city, an entire line of enemy archers cornered Joan.

A man pulled her from her horse.

She knew she would die at their hand.

The Burgundians held Joan hostage for six months. When ransom negotiations with a bishop were met, Joan climbed her tower in an attempt to escape. Against the wishes of the saints, she flew like a bird through the clouds. And even though she survived the sixty-foot fall, she remained a hostage. Armed with fifty men, the enemies moved her to a new castle.

To be tried as a heretic.

England paid for the trial, and men of the Catholic Church questioned Joan for a year. For heresy—going against the church and government. For wearing men's clothing to protect herself.

Though she was clever and smart with her answers, she was found guilty and sentenced to life in prison. She signed a paper saying she would never commit the crimes again. But when the guards stole her feminine clothes, she was forced to again wear her battle garments.

The court declared this a relapse of heresy, and she was sentenced to death.

The next morning, they brought Joan to the public stake to be burned. The crowd cheered and called her a witch. Joan prayed and kissed a handmade cross. When they lit the wood below her feet, she called out for Jesus six times. That was it.

When it was over, her ashes drifted down the River Seine.

22

By the end of the day, it's really hot, hovering at one hundred degrees when we leave the library. I watch the water out the car window, the sun making it white and sharp, and put my head against the door. I close my eyes. That heavy feeling never left me, not all afternoon.

"Mary, you should tell your mom what you're doing," Betty says. "She was enthralled with NASA and exploration when we were little and wanted to be an astronaut. She wanted to go to space camp. Maybe you two have more in common than you think."

I doubt that. What if she tells my dad? What if she forces me to stop because I'm friends with Kip? "Maybe." I keep my eyes on the road ahead of us. The pavement gives off little heat ripples.

"Talk to your mother. Tell her what you're doing. Isn't that easier?"

When Joan told her parents she wanted to join the military, her father threatened to throw her in the river. She couldn't swim.

I think about it as we pull in front of Ford's, my eyebrows pushed down. "I don't know." Maybe I'm just cautious. Maybe it's because I have no idea how she'll react. Maybe, and this is the worst thought of all, it's because she won't care.

"I'll see you in the morning," Betty says.

When Betty pulls out of the driveway, I turn and look at the cottage. Everything looks normal on the outside, and I feel like if the cottage is fine, the sub should be fine. I know I'm wrong though.

A hollow feeling forms in my chest. I've felt this way before.

I don't go to Mr. Jack's. I don't ask for a key. I step around the side of the cabin, the hollow feeling pooling, spilling around my feet like sloshing water.

I choke in air.

The sub is propped on its lift like usual, but the porthole has a crack down the center of the glass.

On top, the hatch is torn off and hanging awkwardly, barely connected. I press my hands to my chest, then fumble for my Joan card. I have no idea where it is. I haven't thought about it in days. It might be in my room. It might be at Lydia's. *Where is it?*

I pull out my phone and send a message. *Can you come to Ford's? Right now?*

I crumple on the ground, the concrete cool despite the heat. I fold myself into a ball and close my eyes.

A few minutes, or maybe hours or days, later, I feel someone kneel next to me. "Murph? What's going on?"

I sit up. Kip is warm, his shoulder touching mine. Like he carried the hot sun under the shade of the porch. My stomach lurches. I have to tell him.

"He did it," I say. "He found out about the sub, and he wrecked it." I say the words I wish weren't true. They float out of me. Drift far away. Across the Bay. Across the world.

"Who?" Kip's voice changes. "Your dad? Why would he do that?"

I raise my chin. "Because it was mine." Because I was happy.

I try not to cry. Joan wouldn't cry. My chest aches, and it comes from so far down in me, it terrifies me. "He did it before," I say. "In third grade, before I went to stay with Betty, before the social worker came. The tires on my mom's car went missing. All four of them just disappeared." My eyes burn while I talk. "And she cried really hard on her bed, so I curled up next to her and cried too. But I didn't really understand, because they were just tires."

"But they weren't just tires."

"She was trying to leave." Only, she couldn't.

"I'm sorry, Mary," Kip says. And I believe him. "We

can fix it," he says gently. "We can replace the porthole and solder the hatch again. You can wear that helmet you hate so much."

He's trying to get me to laugh. But I can't. My father stole my tires. I'm going to be just like my mother. I'll be stuck here my whole life. I'll never do anything. Certainly won't pilot a sub.

"Should we call someone? The police? Ford?" he asks.

I shake my head. The police have never helped my mother once.

Kip stands up. "I hate him." He goes over to Ford's tools and pulls out a wrench. I watch him unhinge the hatch and remove the broken glass. He sweeps it into a dustpan and throws it in the garbage. I can't move. I can only watch.

I am underwater.

And I am drowning.

Kip's phone buzzes three times while he's putting the hatch on top of a work bench. He sighs. "I gotta go. Everyone's out on the water because of the heat."

Even in the shade, his shirt is soaked with sweat and his hairline is damp.

"Do you want to walk with me? I don't . . ." He rubs the back of his neck. "We can fix this."

I don't know. I don't know if I can fix this.

"I'm going to stay here for a little bit," I say. "Kip?" My voice sounds like it belongs to someone else. "Thank you for coming."

When he leaves, I slump back down on the concrete.

It takes me a long time to move. Hours. I leave the safety of Ford's cabin. I find myself at the Cliffs, but my body doesn't feel light and floaty looking at the water. It feels numb.

The walk home is boiling. When I hit Our Lady, I see sheriff lights at the marina. I freeze. The lights spin, bouncing colors against the white paint of the building. The sirens don't sound. I can't look over; my stomach's on fire.

Maybe some waterman got sick from the heat, that's all. Maybe an older waterman, I tell myself. Probably Buddy. Try to convince the tremble in my thoughts.

I wring my hands together. It doesn't feel right.

My heart racing, I walk into the house, sit at the kitchen table, and stand up again. I pour myself a glass of water and sit back down, fidgety. The house is overwhelmingly quiet. The air feels like static. I tap my fingers against the glass.

The screen door bursts open, and I expect to see my mom, but when I turn, Lydia is flying toward me.

"Come quick! It's Kip!"

I don't understand. I just saw him. I just saw Kip. He has to be fine. Fine. "Kip?"

"Why didn't you answer your phone? I swear!"

"Why?" The word is hooked to my throat.

"Your dad . . . Kip." She's having a hard time speaking and bends over, her hands on her knees.

"What about them?" My stomach clenches. I don't want to know.

"Your dad went to the marina. Kip's hurt."

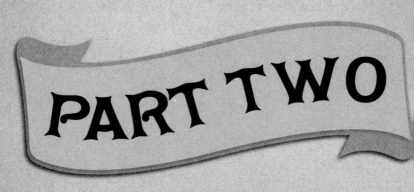

PART TWO

SURFACING

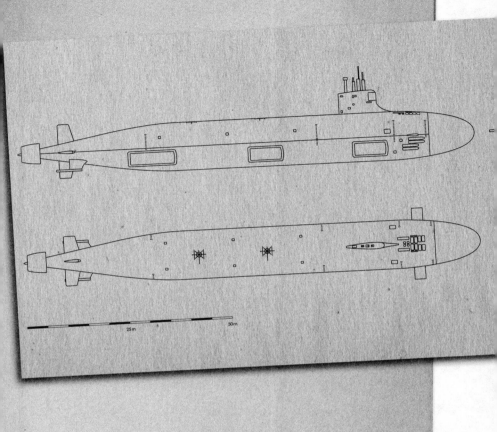

Forward boldly!

—The battle cry of St. Joan of Arc

23

Hail Mary, full of grace. The Lord is with thee. Blessed art thou among women and blessed is the fruit of thy womb, Jesus. Holy Mary, mother of God, pray for us sinners, now and at the hour of our death. Amen.

I pray as I run. I run as I pray. It takes me nine Hail Marys to get to the marina.

When I was little, I would take baths—my parents fighting in the other room—and slip my head under the surface. The water muffled their voices echoing in my brain.

Everything is loud and muffled now. The cars. The blinking of the squad car. People on the boardwalk gawking. It's all too loud.

And it's so, so hot. My mouth is dry, but everything else in the world, it seems, is covered in liquid. My shirt sticks to my ribs, and when I pull on it, the sweat makes it cling to me more.

I stop when I hit the doorstep. A chum bucket filled with cement props the door open. Noisy fans whir in each corner of the bait shop section of the marina. There's no happy ding of the door or a smiling little Dwyer sister with a face full of freckles.

Kip's mom is standing behind the counter, next to a wall of hooks, in a dress the color of sunshine and with her teased, bleached hair. She looks out of place. Too bright. Too sunny for a dire day.

Mrs. Dwyer is speaking to a police officer, someone from the sheriff's department, and he writes down everything she says. When she sees me walk in, she stops talking. The expression on her tan face is blank, like she doesn't recognize me.

I don't know what to say, so I stand there and wait, the last few minutes rushing in like a flood. Finally, Mrs. Dwyer makes a decision and points. I follow her direction and walk to the back of the store, into a little room where they sell ice cream and soda.

One fan, cranked high, points at me and buzzes in my ears.

Kip sits on a metal folding chair, with his dad standing behind him. They're both looking at Dr. Lewis, the ancient island doctor.

Kip holds a towel pressed to his face, and blood spots it like the bottom of my dad's boat, bright red and wet. Blooms of crimson. He sees me and puts the towel in his lap. He tries to stand, but winces and sits back down. A busted nose and a split bottom lip.

Such a nice mouth, and now it's ruined.

My dad did that.

I can't move. My feet are glued to the floor. I want to vomit. I think I might. Mr. Dwyer starts to walk toward me, but I turn and bolt.

I run out the main store and into the parking lot, lean against the building, and sink. I stay there until I hear Lydia's voice.

"Mary!"

I pick up my head. She and Omar stand in front of me, the brilliant red of the sunset behind them. The same color as Kip's towel.

"Why are you out here?"

I shrug.

"Did you see him? Is he here? The hospital?" She spits out questions as fast as her brain can think them.

Mine can't keep up. "What?"

"Did you see Kip?" she asks, slowing down, sitting next to me in the gravel.

I nod.

"Is he okay?" Omar asks.

"I don't know." My words are slow, so slow.

"Why don't you know?" Lydia speeds up again. "What does she mean?" she asks Omar. She stands. "We're going in there."

I don't even watch them go. I just keep staring ahead. I feel sick.

I get up. I'm a rockfish, a hook in my mouth, being dragged. First, I'm pulled to my house, onto my bike. And then I'm reeled in, flying from the marina. Gasping for air.

My despair pedals my feet and brings me to the Cliffs. I climb and stand at the top, watching the water below. I stand there a long time, the waves light and free under me.

My dad hits. His fists are heavy and binding. He hits my mom. He hits me. He hit the bartender at the Tavern. He hit an inmate the last time he was in prison and had to stay longer. He's never hit my friend before, though. Guilt runs through me. It's my fault.

If I had been at the marina. If I hadn't told Kip. If we weren't working on the sub.

I sob into the wind.

I shake my head and look down at the water. No. *No.* That's what he does. Makes it feel like it's your fault. When the blame is always his. *Always.*

I want to feel light and free like the waves.

I scramble down the side of the Cliffs. At the water's edge, I stick my toes in. The brackish water licks my ankles. I walk out until the surface hits my shorts. My waist.

It's just like the bathtub. Just like it. That's what I tell myself. It's a few feet deep. I won't drown.

I sink down with a huge sigh. A cry out. He hurt my friend. A boy I like. He ruined my sub. I clench my fists and press them against my chin. I don't know if Kip is okay. I don't know if he'll ever talk to me again. I don't know anything.

This is what I get. This is what I get for trying to escape. For liking a boy. For handing someone my heart.

I shake my fingers out, make my mouth a circle, and blow hard. I will not let my father pull me under.

When I'm ready, I fill my lungs and lie on the water like a bed, my arms outstretched, my body a *t*. I panic, once, and stick a foot firmly back down in the sand. But then I let go. I point my chest to the sky. My hair swirls around me.

And I'm floating light and free in the Bay.

24

I walk home soaked, but I don't mind because it's so hot. Even though it's dark, the heat lingers. Clings tight to the Bay. My mother is waiting for me at the kitchen table when I open the door. "I guess you heard about your dad."

I don't want to talk about him. I want to drink my water and go to sleep. Tomorrow I have work at the library. And I am so, so exhausted.

"Yes." I pour myself water at the sink. "How long this time?" I sit across from her. My body is tired. We've had this conversation before, and it leaves me emotionless.

"I don't know. He's still in jail. I won't be able to make bail for at least a month. And then there will be a trial," she says. "I'll need you to check some of the crab pots this weekend." Mom tucks her frazzled hair behind her ear and stands, putting her dirty dish in the sink.

A month. All of July. I have a month to finish the sub without worrying if he'll ruin it. Without worrying he'll find out and hurt someone again.

"It was that Dwyer boy's fault," Mom whispers.

I pull my wet hair off my neck. "Why do you keep calling him that?" It's annoying me, makes my skin itchy. "We've known him my whole life. It's Kip."

"Fine. Kip." She says it like the word is disgusting. "Kip started it." She props her arms on the counter behind her.

The water gets stuck in my throat. "I doubt that."

"That's what Buddy told me."

Buddy. Buddy barely knows what day it is. I scowl. But he was probably at the marina earlier. "Why would Buddy say that?"

"Because it's true." She waves her hands around. "Your dad just went to gas up the boat."

I'm quiet, thinking, trying to figure it out. But the air is so hot. "Why would Dad be in jail then?"

"Because *Kip*"—the word as sharp as the knives in the drawers behind her—"is a minor. And your dad's got priors."

If I think clearly about it, my eyes closed, I know Kip didn't start anything, that he would never hurt someone. He may have said something rude or inappropriate to my dad. I would bet money on that. But Kip wouldn't put his hands on anyone in anger.

Last year, two baseball players got in a fight in the cafeteria, and one pinned the other on top of a table. Kip and Omar split them up before the teachers could reach them. That's who that Dwyer boy is.

I know where the blame sits.

"Like you start fights with Dad, Mom? Like I do? It's our fault, right?"

I don't wait for her to respond. In my room, I lock the door and lean against it, staring at the model on my desk that Kip and I made. I wonder if he's home. If he blames me. If he hates me.

I pull out the phone Betty got me and look at the screen. Missed calls from Lydia that I didn't hear when I silenced it to go to the Murphy house. The afternoon bangs into me again, and my fingers shake.

I'm sorry, I text him.

But I don't hear anything back. I stare at the ceiling for hours, trying to sleep. But the day creeps into my brain, making it difficult to rest. When I wake up in the morning, no reply lights my screen. I get ready early, before Betty picks me up. I need to talk to him. I have to see how he's doing.

Two pickup trucks are in the marina parking lot. No police cars. Kip's mom is behind the counter again, the one person in the store. Voices on the dock outside drift in.

"Umm, hi, Mrs. Dwyer," I say.

She doesn't answer me at first, just looks, assessing. She probably wants to toss me overboard, a humane catch-and-release. "Mary," she says finally.

"Is Kip around?"

"No." Her jaw tightens. "Dr. Lewis told him no work for a week. He wanted him to stay overnight at the hospital." The hospital's up at North Beach, near the library. It's not on the island.

I watch her cotton-candy hair. "Do you know where I could find him?"

When she doesn't answer, I squirm like I've never squirmed before. "I'm not really sure what happened yesterday, but I'm sorry. I feel responsible."

She narrows her eyes. "You should."

I tug on a strand of my hair. "Could I talk to Kip about it?"

"He's at home." She crosses her arms over her polka-dot dress. "After what your father did." She says it like I did it, like I hit Kip.

"Thank you, ma'am."

The Dwyer house is behind Our Lady and the marina, in a little corner of the Bay. It's large and white and wooden with a big porch across the front. I knock on the door and wait. Barbara answers and stands staring at me, just like her mother did. The Dwyer ladies are terrifying.

"Babe, can I talk to Kip?" Shrimp runs to the door and licks my hand, her tail and butt moving wildly. At least she's happy to see me.

"I don't think he wants to see you," she says softly.

"Why?" I squeak.

She raises her shoulders.

I peek in the house. "Can you check?"

Barbara turns on one foot, leaves the door cracked, and yells at Shrimp not to run outside. I wait and stare at the gold crab knocker, twisting my hands together and flipping Shrimp's ear when she presses her face against me.

Babe comes back and leans against the door. "He said he's sleeping."

"He *said* it?" I should have known. I should have realized he wouldn't want to see me. Why would he?

I'm a Murphy.

25

I walk back to my house with my arms wrapped tight. With watery eyes, I wait outside until Betty pulls in.

She gets out of the car when she sees me. "Do you want to stay home?"

I shake my head and press my lips together.

"Is this about your dad and your boy? Your mother told me." She adjusts her glasses.

I nod and wipe my eyes. My mother and Betty talk?

"You look terrible."

Thanks. "I want to go to the library. I don't want to stay here." I open the car door and sit.

The ride is quiet. Aunt Betty doesn't turn on NPR. I lean my head against the window. "Is it because I'm a Murphy?" I ask her.

"Is what?"

"Do you think Kip doesn't like me because I'm a Murphy? I'm tainted." Everything that can go wrong, will. I should have known. It was practically written in my stars. It's a bad smell that clings to hair, the Murphy name.

Betty makes a weird noise in her throat and watches me out of the side of her glasses. "Why do you think that?"

I tell her everything. I tell her about Kip. And his face. And how he won't talk to me. My stomach hurts when I say it all.

Betty frowns. "I don't know much about teenage boys, but he might be embarrassed."

I wipe my nose and smooth my hair the closer we get to the library. "Why would he be embarrassed?"

"Well, he likes you. And your dad beat him up? He's probably feeling a lot of emotions over that. And boys are taught some problematic lessons about what it means to be a man. Give him some time. Let his bruises heal. Let his ego do the same. If he's smart, he'll come around."

I don't have time. I have a month to get this done. To build and pilot the sub before my father gets back and ruins everything. Before Ford leaves for Japan. We were so close, and now the porthole and hatch are damaged. Now Kip hates me.

I am distracted all day. My brain is cloudy. Foggy like the dawn. I count down the hours until I can get to the cottage to work on the sub. Kip was supposed to help. Now I'm not so sure. I check my phone every few minutes. Nothing.

Five old women want to print emails. One man needs help with a job application. At lunch, I eat only my pretzels. I leave my sandwich in its bag. The jam leaks out, a dark purple ooze. The thin skin next to Kip's eye might be that color right now. I sigh and wipe salt off my lip.

Betty tells me about the July theme for the children's section: Dissent Is Patriotic. She made a poster, a bright red fist blazing defiantly. Her cheeks flush with excitement while she talks about it.

At the end of the day, when Betty drops me off at Ford's, I get serious in the car. "Thanks, Aunt Betty."

"No problem, kid. I like driving."

"No, I mean for everything. Driving and giving me a job. A phone. You've been really good to me, and I don't deserve it." I look down at my hands.

"You deserve kindness, just like everyone else in this world. You're just not used to it, and that's a crying shame. I should have done this earlier." She hands me my backpack. "You are worthy, Mary."

"Worthy of what?" My heart feels like it's been split open. I can't tell if that's a good thing or not. Feeling so much. All I've done is feel lately.

"Everything, honey. Happiness. Love. You deserve it all. Your parents forgot to tell you that." I remember now. Staying with Aunt Betty in third grade at the hotel across from the fire station. We ordered pizza, and I picked the peppers off. She said she would order without peppers the next time.

No one's ever told me I deserve happiness before.

26

In the cottage, Ford and I work on the inside equipment. I searched online and found a medical absorbent that will clean my exhaled carbon dioxide. It's called Sodasorb. It looks like kitty litter and when it absorbs my air, it changes color. We attach a small fan to a bucket of it. When the marine batteries are hooked up, the sub will power the fan.

While my face is down, Ford says, "Do you want to talk about yesterday?"

I shake my head. "It was my dad. But he's in jail now."

Ford sighs. He might already know. The island is small. No one else's father is getting arrested all the time. Only mine.

"I had an angry father," he says. "That's why I joined the Navy. I could never really be myself around him. I felt like two different people. I suppose I still do."

I don't say anything, only readjust the fan. I think the sweet Ford is the real version. Maybe I'm the same way. I'm not sure.

"He hurt Kip. That's why he's not here today." My throat burns.

"Oh," Ford says, rubbing his jaw. "That I was unaware of."

"He probably hates me."

"Oh, Miss Mary, we are not our parents, and your Mr. Kip is very aware of that."

For the next week, Ford asks me if Kip is coming, and each time, I tell him no. I wish he would listen the first time. Lydia and Omar haven't seen him either. I miss him. I don't think he'll ever forgive me.

On the seventh day without Kip, Ford says, "We need those marine batteries." He watches me. Lets his meaning settle.

I'm making weight adjustments on the CAD program. A version of the propane tank chugs across the screen. "I know."

"I could go down to the marina, or someone else could . . ." Ford speaks slowly.

I glare at him. "I know what you're doing."

He laughs and shakes his head.

"Fine!" I stand up fast and close the program angrily. "I'll go. It's my job anyway."

"You know the old saying about catching more flies with honey?"

I push my eyebrows down. "Yes. That's never really been my specialty."

"Well, make it your specialty, darlin'. And go fix your hair." He shakes his head at me again and waves a screwdriver wildly in the air.

I stomp off to the bathroom, dodging textbooks on thermo engineering and economics. "I don't even need Kip. You're annoying enough for the both of you."

I look in the mirror. My hair is loose and wild. I turn on the faucet and wet my hand, smoothing my curls as best I can. I think about when Kip woke me up in the middle of the night to show me the USS *New York*. Frowning, I turn off the water. I need to apologize. I bite the inside of my mouth.

It's getting dark as I head into Bournes. The sky reflects purple on the water, and the bridge is loud with lit cars passing over. The boardwalk is busy with kids playing and adults walking. I avoid eyes and slip into the store.

The bell dings when I step in, and Kip's behind the counter. He's the only one here.

"Hi," I say, and remembering what Ford said, I push my hair behind my ears and try to smile.

"Hey."

There's a long pause, and I feel incredibly awkward. I tap my fingers against the linoleum countertop. "Umm, I need three marine batteries."

He pulls them off the wall. They're a lot bigger than I expected. "Anything else?" he asks, putting them between us.

"Not right now."

He scans them, and I hand him my money. All my money, it feels like. I pass it over hesitantly, and when he gives me coins back, I jam them in my pocket. Everything feels too weird. I wish there were people in the store or that he would call me Murph or make a joke.

Two bruises line his nose, yellow skin and red scabs. Caution and stop. I bet everyone's asking him about it, and he has to explain. Maybe his friends are teasing him. I want to brush the bruises away. They're there because of me.

"Can I leave these here and pick them up tomorrow?" I ask. "I didn't bring anything to carry them."

"Sure. I'll leave a note for Babe." He taps one of them with his thumb.

The bell rings on the door, and we both watch his dad walk into the shop. Mr. Dwyer is a big, handsome man with red hair. He's talking to a young woman in a bathing suit, and they don't acknowledge us.

I turn back to Kip, who is still looking at them. He sticks his thumbnail in his mouth and bites.

I don't know what to do. I have to apologize, even if Kip's dad is a cheater. I close my eyes. *Do it, Murphy. Apologize.*

Mr. Dwyer tells Kip to go home for dinner, and he and the girl move into the other half of the store. Gross. I'm annoyed for Kip. "Are you okay?" I ask him.

"Because of that?" He points after them. "I'm sure it's totally work-related," he jokes. Kip arranges the batteries in a straight row, pushing them together, and sweeps off the top of the counter with his hand. "He's a good dad but a bad husband."

"Do you want to talk about it?"

"I'm fine," he says. He kind of smiles. "Do you want to talk about your dad?"

"No." Not one bit. I shake my head. "But I think I need to." I keep my eyes down. "I'm sorry. About everything. I'm sorry he did that to you." I look at his face. "I'm sorry I ran out of here."

This is hard. So hard. Murphys don't apologize. At least, I've never heard them do it.

"Okay," he says. What does "okay" mean? Okay, he forgives me? I have no clue. He rubs the back of his neck, and I watch the freckles on his hand. Last week, we were hugging. We were holding hands. And now . . .

"We made a carbon dioxide thing to clean the air in the sub," I blurt out. "So I don't die. Hopefully." I make the sign of the cross.

"That's cool." He smiles back. It's something. I want to jump over the counter and squeeze him with a hug, but I attempt to keep it together.

"If you want to come back. If you want to work on it . . ." I scrunch my face. "I miss . . ."

He looks around the store. "Maybe I could drop off the batteries tomorrow."

It's not a joke. He doesn't say, "You miss me, Murph, because I'm so hot? Because you're in love with me?" But it's something.

I don't want to push him. "Yeah," I say. "Up to you!"

~~~~~~~~~~~~~~~~~~~~~~~~~~~

The next afternoon, I'm nervous. Even though it's only 4:30, and too early for Kip to leave the marina, I watch the door obsessively. Like a dog, I perk up at each little noise. Comparing yourself to a dog is never a good sign. Ford watches my bouncing leg.

"He'll be here," he says. Like he can predict the future.

"How do you know?"

"He'll be here. Work on that." Ford points to the list on my lap. I have to weigh each piece of the equipment and everything I'll take in the sub, including me and the clothes I'll wear. The weight needs to be accounted for and exactly the same the day of the launch. The total has to equal the water displaced. To reach neutral buoyancy, they have to balance each other out.

I weigh equipment until 6:30, making changes on the computer, and check the door while Ford makes dinner. I haven't eaten at my own house in weeks and wonder if my mom even notices. I haven't seen her since my dad was arrested.

At 7:30, I can't handle it anymore. I can't focus. I watch the door and stand up. If there were room in the clutter, I would pace.

"He's not coming." I bite the inside of my mouth. Joan of Arc probably never had to deal with this.

"We can do it ourselves."

Where did his optimism go? I can't stay here waiting. Maybe I'll go to the Cliffs. I owe Mr. Jack some shark teeth.

There's a small knock on the screen door, and I look over at Ford. He raises his eyebrows and waves his hands for me to answer it. After maneuvering around the mess, I open the door and feel immediate relief.

Kip.

Except Kip won't talk to me. Ford hands him a lukewarm plate of what we just ate—sausage and salad—and Kip devours it in the kitchen. But he will only look at Ford.

I stand next to the table and tell him, "Our practice launch is in two weeks!"

He keeps his eyes on Ford and grunts.

So I try again. "We got a buoy that will float above me, tethered to the sub, so you can see where I am in the water."

"Okay," he says, his eyes on his fork.

I scowl. *What is going on?* Kip usually talks too much. Makes everything a joke. This is not Kip Dwyer.

For the whole night, he ignores me, and I bite my lip and stare at the back of his head when he laughs with Ford. And then a whole week goes by like that. I am confused. So confused. I thought him coming to the cottage meant everything was okay, or at least, getting better.

I have help with the sub, but my friend is gone.

∿∿∿∿∿∿∿∿∿∿∿∿∿∿∿∿∿∿∿∿∿

The week before the practice launch, I go to Lydia's to spend the night. Her house is the same size and shape as mine, but it feels younger, newer. Fresh paint on the walls and shiny, wooden floors. Nothing's cracked or peeling.

But it does smell like vinegar and cabbage. The counter is covered in jars and cutting boards full of shredded vegetables. Lydia's mother is making sauerkraut, mashing it with salt. She's white and German, and Lydia's dad is black and American. They met when he was stationed in Germany. Lydia thinks they're too controlling, but they just love her and her older brother a lot.

Lydia runs down the stairs when she hears me come in. She's wearing shorts and a big T-shirt with old cartoons.

"Mom!" She groans. "It smells so bad in here."

Her mother clucks her tongue and says, "Go outside, then." She sounds like she's from Bournes.

"Do you want to go to the beach?" Lydia asks me.

"No." I know I don't really have a choice.

Lydia rolls her eyes. "Come on, let's get our suits on." She pulls me by the arm. "Because I can't get any work done when it smells like this in here!" she tells her mom. I love them. I don't love the beach.

In her room, I stand over her set, looking at the clay dragon. She's made individual scales on his belly. "How's the animation?" I ask while she changes.

"Terrible. Barry's friends were over last night, and they make so much noise." Her brother is home from college. Lydia throws a swimsuit at my head. "I don't want to talk about that. Tell me about Kip. How's his face?"

I frown. "It's healing? I don't know. He still won't talk to me." I turn my back to her and pull on her old red bathing suit.

"What?"

I finish changing and flop on her bed, my hair making a cloud. "He's probably never going to talk to me again."

"That's not true." She lies down too. "Man, every time I think you two are gonna get together, you don't. And then I'm stuck double-dating with the baseball girlfriends." Lydia elbows me. "Think of me, Mary. Think of me."

I tip my head to face her and smile as she gets up.

"Let's go!" she says. "I'm gonna start gagging. The smell of cabbage when it's a million degrees outside, what is wrong with her?"

⁓⁓⁓⁓⁓⁓⁓⁓⁓⁓⁓⁓⁓⁓⁓⁓⁓⁓⁓⁓⁓⁓⁓⁓

I go to sleep with burnt shoulders. In the morning, I go to Ford's. Kip shows up, not talking to me still, but joking with Ford about the state of the living room. I glare at him.

"Okay, you two," Ford says. "I am sick of this lovers' quarrel."

I wrinkle my nose. What a gross word. For the first time in forever, Kip and I look at each other and smile.

"Outside. Outside." He shoos us toward the door. "Go figure this out. I will not have this negative energy under my roof, y'all." The more adamant he gets, the more southern he sounds.

Outside is hot. The crickets chirp in the tall grass behind the sub. On the water, a boat starts, a water-skier in tow. I squirm.

"It doesn't look damaged now," Kip says.

I put my hand on the metal. "Mr. Jack replaced the glass." I push gravel around with my shoe. "We have to waterproof the seams with marine epoxy, but . . ." I trail off. Are we really going to talk about the sub?

Kip grabs Ford's stool and plants it next to the sub. He climbs up and cranks the handle to the hatch. It doesn't look easy to do, and because he's bigger than I am, I worry I won't be able to do it.

Peering down, he says, "It's pretty dark down there."

"Let's hope. It wouldn't be good if there were holes in the metal, would it?" I laugh to myself and fidget. Before everything bad happened, we hugged. Does he want to hug again? I do. My heart thumps faster thinking about it.

"Hey, I'm supposed to be the funny one." He pulls his head out, his blond hair bright. "You're doing a great job, Murph."

The compliment makes me switch the weight on my feet. He's acting normal. He called me Murph.

He steps down from the stool and stands in front of me. His white T-shirt is new and smells clean. "In two weeks, you're going to pilot across the Bay."

I have to squint to see him, the sun is so strong. "That's the scary part." I laugh and wrap my hands behind my back.

"Too scary for me, but you're brave."

I don't know how to tell him what that means to me. He keeps getting closer to me, and I think all my organs have liquefied. It must be the fabric softener. That's why his shirt smells like that. I want to hug him again. I want to kiss him.

Wait a minute. Five minutes ago, I thought he was mad at me. I rub my forehead. "You're not mad at me anymore?"

"What?" Kip tilts his head and steps back. "I wasn't mad at you. You were mad at me."

"No," I say. "That's not true. Why would I be angry with you?"

"Because you said your dad couldn't go back to . . ." He pauses. "Jail." He whispers it. "And then—"

"No." I fold my arms. "I feel like I can breathe when he's gone." I've never told anyone that. But I don't understand. "You haven't talked to me all week."

"You didn't talk to me!"

When I stare up at him, he says, "Okay, maybe it was me. I cussed at your dad when he came to the marina. I'm sorry. I feel like I started it." He looks up at the sky, and I can see the whites of his eyes. "And I was embarrassed you saw my dad."

I hug him like I did on Lydia's porch. It feels so long ago. I might be a different person. "You shouldn't be embarrassed. Or sorry. You're not your dad. And I'm not mine."

28

At the library the next morning, I smile while Betty's voice sounds through the walls during story time. Distracted, I read about high-gauge wires. I need to replace the weaker wire on the fan with them. When we attached the batteries last night, the fan burned out because they weren't durable enough.

In the afternoon, I'm still smiling. Thinking about hugging. About laundry detergent. About Kip Dwyer. Betty knocks on the doorway of the lab. "There's a man here to see you."

I frown and sit up straight, no longer grinning to myself. I know who it is. "Harris?" I sigh.

Betty looks surprised, her eyebrows above the rim of her glasses. "Yes, how did you know?"

I roll my eyes. "Social worker."

"Should I let him in?"

"Okay."

Mr. Harris's face appears where Betty's was, and I just watch him. He walks in, surveys the room, and pulls out a swivel chair.

"Mary," he says, sitting perpendicular to me, a line of sweat on his forehead. "I thought I'd catch up with you today."

"You always find me."

"I'm like James Bond." He chuckles.

As a reply, I frown at the computer screen ahead of me.

"I saw your father's name in the police blotter."

My eyes as far away from his as I can get them, I say, "Yes."

"And something about a minor?"

"Not me," I say quickly. "I'm not the minor." It's an old habit to protect him. But I don't like it. It's like a curve in a mirror that makes your reflection distorted.

"Okay, then who was the minor he assaulted?" Mr. Harris shifts in the chair.

I play with the nail on my thumb and weigh out my options. Social workers always act like if you just talk, everything will be solved. If you just tell, spill, pour out, they can fix your world with a magic wand. Wave it across your life and set it right. But that's not how it works.

What happens when you tell the truth is change. Change you can't control. Change that makes every decision for you.

But now I feel a narrow little nagging. He broke my submersible. He hurt my friend. The truth wrestles inside me, begging to escape.

"Kip," I finally tell him.

Mr. Harris looks shocked that I provided information. He flips through the pages of my file. "Kip is from the base incident?"

I nod.

"And why would your father do that?"

Because I was trying to get away and Kip was helping me. Because Kip knows what kind of person Robert Murphy is. Because Kip stood up for me.

Mr. Harris asks so nicely, but my words don't want to come out anymore. What would they do with me? Where would I go? And he hurt Kip once. Who knows what he'll do next. "He's in jail, Mr. Harris. He's not home. I'm fine. Everything is fine."

"How about we try a different approach, Mary? Did you feel safe when your father was home?"

"I barely saw him. He was on the water a lot." More protection. It spits out of my mouth involuntarily. It's a reflex. It's the doctor hitting my knee and my leg kicking out.

"But when you did. When you were at home, and he was?"

I know if I say, "Yes, I feel safe," Mr. Harris will leave me alone. He will disappear until the next storm. But if I say, "No, I never feel safe," my life will change.

I squirm. I can't lie. And I can't tell the truth.

"Are you staying at home?" He asks so gently, I feel like I've let him down.

"Yes." Most of the time.

"I only want to help," he says. "I can't help unless you tell me something." He hands me another bent white card. The other one is in my desk at home. Just in case. "If you ever change your mind or need to talk, you call me, no matter what."

When I don't reach for the card, he puts it next to the keyboard.

"It's great you're spending time here. Your aunt seems like a wonderful lady. It's good to have people like her in your life."

When he leaves, Betty comes back to the computer lab. She drinks from her water bottle. "What was he here for?" she asks.

"Dad." I wrap a piece of hair around my fingertip, thinking.

My aunt tips her head to the side. "What kind of questions do social workers ask?"

"If I feel safe. Stuff like that."

"Do you?"

I scratch my temple. "Feel safe?" I pause. No. "I don't know. I feel safe here and at Ford's and school. And Lydia's. I always feel safe there." Tears start to fill my eyes, so I blink them away. "I feel like Mom and I are always waiting. For the next explosion or when he comes home. I can never relax." My voice is doing funny things, and I have to wipe my eyes.

"Did you tell Mr. Harris that?" Betty squats down and holds my hand.

"No."

"Why not?"

"I just . . ." I put my head in my hands.

"You shouldn't have to feel afraid all the time, Mary." Betty's gruff voice is soft. "I know change is hard, but I've offered this to your mother before. I didn't want to rush you or force you into anything. But if you would like to live with me, with us, we would love to have you."

Change. Too much change. Would I leave the Bay? Leave Our Lady? Leave Lydia and Kip? And what would happen to my mother? What would my father do? Who would he punish?

I can't. I can't do it.

29

"What do you want to do for your birthday?" Lydia asks me two days later.

"I don't know." I do know. My birthday is in two days, and the only thing I can think about is kissing. That's all I want to do, and I've decided I'm going to do it on my birthday. I'm going to have my first kiss, and I've scheduled it like a dentist appointment.

"Do you want to go to the beach for it?"

"No. Not at all."

Lydia's crouched in the corner of her bedroom, bending over her set and mumbling to herself. She's shaping flowers, little yellow petals that will push a sword out of the ground. "I haven't figured out the ending," she says. "And I think I should have done that first."

"What do you mean?"

"Like I want to make a point, you know? Before, I wasn't telling stories. I was only making scenes." In seventh grade, Lydia made an apple unpeeling and clouds floating across a blue sky. This year, she got a nice camera for her birthday and started doing entire scenes, a monster going to the grocery store, a mermaid diving into water.

"And now I don't want the ending to be cliché. Like I don't want her to tame the dragon. That's been done. I don't want a knight to slay him." Lydia crosses her arms over her knees and groans, yellow clay petals in her hand. "And killing the dragon makes me a little sad."

She picks up the dragon that's perched on the edge of her desk and examines the body, white and gray with black horns on each side of its head.

"Sometimes dragons need to be slayed," I say.

~~~~~~~~~~~~~~~~~~~~~~~~~~

We put the motor together and attach it to the sub on Sunday. I use the last of my money to buy a trolling motor at Kip's store, and even with the Dwyer family discount, I'm broke until I get paid in two weeks.

Ford walks to a neighbor's cottage to borrow a large trash can to test the motor in water, and Kip and I wait in the driveway, next to the sub.

"I asked my dad if we could take the boat out for your birthday." He says it halfway between a statement and a question.

"That sounds like fun," I tell him. I'm having a hard time concentrating when he's around, and working on the sub would be less distracting if he weren't here. But I want him here. It's confusing.

"Lydia wants to go too. And then probably Omar." Another half question.

I can feel him reading my face. "Okay."

"Do you want to go the same route across the Bay as the sub?"

To the Eastern Shore. "Work and pleasure?" I say. Oh Lord. I lean against the sub, pretending to be relaxed. *Don't say anything about Joan of Arc. Don't do it, Murphy.*

"I kinda wish they weren't going with us, but Lydia's your best friend." He puts his hand on my arm, and I will myself not to get goose bumps.

It takes me a minute to get my voice to work. "She is." The smaller my sentences, the better. Then I won't say anything too weird.

He takes off his hand and laughs. "Plus, Joan of Arc. Who do you like the best? Lydia, Joan, or me?"

I scowl at him. He's always teasing me. He probably will when we kiss. If we kiss. "Definitely not you."

My birthday is July 16, which means I never get a school birthday. Sometimes the teachers and nuns celebrate it the first week of school, lumped in with the other summer birthdays, but mostly everyone forgets.

Lydia never forgets. She always makes me cupcakes and gets me a present.

I'm not expecting anything from anyone, but I do want that kiss. I agonize over it. How do people know what to do?

Waking up much earlier than usual, I take a long time getting ready. That seems like something I should do. I wash my hair and condition it. Doing everything slowly makes it seem more important.

The phone rings while my head is flipped over. My mom doesn't answer it, so I put my comb down and walk into the kitchen.

On the sixth ring, I pick up and hear my aunt.

"Is everything okay?" I ask immediately, the phone pressed tight to my ear.

"What? Of course, honey. No, no. I just wanted to give you the day off. Have fun with your friends or work on your sub."

"Oh," I say. This changes how I'll spend my day. I wanted to go to the library. Work makes me think about kissing less.

"Happy birthday!" Betty says. "Alex and I will take you out to dinner this weekend, but it's your special day. Go be a teenager."

It's only eight in the morning, so I don't know what to do with myself. At least I know what to do at the library. I'm frowning in the kitchen when my mom walks in.

"Who was that?" she asks, making herself coffee. She doesn't really look at me, and it's the first time we've talked since my dad left.

"Betty. She said I could have the day off."

"What are you going to do? You've been gone a lot lately."

I don't know why she's asking. "Why?" I make myself a sandwich, peanut butter and jelly. I bite into it. It doesn't taste like the homemade blackberry jam that Betty makes.

"Buddy said you've been up with those men at the cottages with that Dwyer boy."

Buddy. Again. And why can't she just say Kip? My hand shakes, and I swallow a bite. "Maybe Buddy should be a private investigator."

"Why have you been there?" she asks.

I'm not telling her. She doesn't care. I shove bite after bite of bread into my mouth.

"And you've spent so much time with Betty."

All the words she's saying bring up different emotions like little bubbles on top of the water. It's what's under the surface that's important. What's making the bubbles? A fish or a shark?

"You probably like her more than us," she says.

More bubbles. We don't usually talk about Betty. And I don't know what to say. I do like Betty. She makes me feel safe and normal. I feel the same at Lydia's and Ford's, really anywhere other than in this house.

I pick up my butter knife and stand at the sink. My hands

vibrate under the running water. I think she wants me to feel bad for her. I can't.

"Mom, you don't care where I am. You never have." My voice is cracking. I'm so angry. I drop the knife in the sink and run from the room, but I only end up in my bedroom. On my bed, I sigh and stare at the ceiling. Even though I've lived here, in this house, in this room, all my life, it's never really felt like mine. This can't be my life here.

The clock on the desk says it's been only ten minutes since Betty called. I sit up and put my hair behind my shoulders. If I pull a strand taut, it reaches all the way to my waist. When I get bored of that, I stare at the phone Betty gave me.

I can't call Lydia because she's probably sleeping. And Kip is working a morning shift because we're going on the boat later. So I call Ford. His greeting sounds groggy, and guilt hits me. I was at his house just twelve hours ago.

"Sorry. My aunt gave me the day off, so I thought I'd come work on the sub."

"Mary, you want to work on the sub?" he asks loudly.

He's acting strange. "Yes."

"I'm not home," he says fast.

"That's okay. I can practice the controls for Saturday." I don't need to go in the house. Even though he's let me go in before when he was gone.

"Umm . . ." He pauses. I hear something fall in the background. "Noon. Can you come at noon?"

"Noon's fine, Ford. Thanks." That means I have hours to waste before I go work. It's so long. I know if I go to the

Cliffs to look for shark teeth, I'll either get too hot and gross for later or wander over to Ford's early. I need to do something else.

I pull out my notes and make a pre- and postlaunch checklist for the practice launch. That takes me thirty minutes. When I'm done, and my mom is gone, I watch TV, but I don't really pay attention. The boat trip is my only thought.

I am going to kiss Kip Dwyer.

∿∿∿∿∿∿∿∿∿∿∿∿∿∿∿∿∿∿∿∿∿∿∿∿

At 11:30, I bolt with my backpack, knowing I'll be early but not caring all that much.

It's hot, and I'm glad I didn't go to the Cliffs. I'd be sweating, my hair ruined. Fifteen minutes later, but fifteen minutes early, I turn my bike down the path to Ford's. I hear a squawk inside that sounds a lot like Lydia.

Weird. They don't know each other. I drop my bike by the screen door and knock.

"I told you she'd be early!"

It *is* Lydia. When I open the door, she's yelling from the living room. Ford and Kip are in the kitchen. Signs and blue streamers hang all over the house. And most shocking of all, the cottage is kind of clean.

"What's going on?" I ask.

"It's your birthday," Lydia says like I don't know. "And now these two are helping, but I think it'd be easier if I did it by myself!" She yells the last part.

"Happy birthday, Miss Mary," Ford drawls from the kitchen. "I'm still finishing up lunch. I'll be there in a minute."

"You didn't need to do this," I tell Lydia as she climbs off a chair, her shorts covered in sky-blue paint.

"Yes, we did. And this isn't even the best part." She switches to a whisper. "Even though we've been cleaning since seven this morning."

"Wait!" Kip says, running into the living room.

"Can I show her?" Lydia asks him, her eyebrows raised and head tipped.

"Sure. I did the hardest part, Murph." Kip crosses his arms, paint on him too, and makes a sneaky face. His usual face.

Lydia's eyes go big and her mouth drops. Her hands on her hips, she says, "He's obviously lying, Mary. You'll know that when you see it."

"Y'all are going to leave me in here?" Ford protests.

"Yes, we are," Kip says.

"I'll get her hands," Lydia says. "Kip, cover her eyes."

"You two are making me nervous," I say, half serious. Kip puts his hands over my eyes and they're rough from the salt water. My heart thumps so loudly, everyone must be able to hear it. He smells like soap. And laundry. And the Bay.

Lydia holds my hand and leads me out of the cottage, slowly, and I take tiny steps so I don't fall. I must look ridiculous.

Then Kip uncovers my eyes and I blink in the sudden sunshine.

"Ta-da! Don't touch it though. It's wet," Lydia says, yelling at Kip, not me.

All I can do is gape.

"What?" Kip asks. "It's not good? Then blame Lydia."

I can't believe I have friends who would do this. They painted my sub. Instead of the old white, it's light blue, and near the hatch, Lydia painted waves crashing. A sword rises out of the water. Joan's sword.

"It's so beautiful." My voice soars away.

"You're gonna slay some dragons," Lydia says.

"It's perfect. I love it." I hug Lydia tight. "Thank you."

"You didn't make any room for me," Kip says. I'm sure he's smirking.

"Shut up," I say, rolling my eyes.

Ford walks out, wiping his hands on a dish towel. "I always miss everything, y'all. What do you think, Miss Mary?"

"It's amazing." I hug him too. "You're all too good to me."

"You still need to name her. We have to register it as a boat with the state of Maryland." He makes quotes with his fingers at the word "boat." "It has to be good. Something with your name or the love of your life."

Kip fake coughs.

I hold my cheeks in so I don't smile. Like I'm in chapel. All the boats at the marina have puns in them. And submarines are usually named after places or war heroes.

Lydia says, "I've got stencils, for when you think of it. We didn't want to do it without you, and I couldn't think of a discreet way to ask. You would've been onto me." She waves the plastic stencils in the air.

I wrap my hair around my finger. I know exactly what I want to call it. "My name," I say. "*Murphy's Law.*"

"What's that?" Lydia asks.

"Whatever can go wrong, will."

"And," Ford butts in, "it's originally a sea term."

"Seems like bad luck, Murph," Kip says. "Shouldn't you name it *Shipwreck* instead?"

I shake my head. "I'm meeting the bad luck head-on." That's the sort of person I want to be.

"I guess athletes have superstitions," he says. He doesn't look convinced though, a frown in the middle of his freckles. I have to look away or our first kiss will be a spectator event.

We eat lunch, blue crab at Ford's dining room table, a piece of craft paper covering the wood. Mallets, knives, and shakers of Old Bay holding it down. I pop the shell off the crab, push aside the lungs, and crack it in half. I always save the claws, the best part, for last.

My three friends laugh around me, and my heart is so happy. Light and free. If Betty were here too, all my favorite people in the whole world would be at this table.

"Dad said we could go at two," Kip tells us.

"About that," Lydia says. "I think I'm done for the day." She gives Ford a fake angry look. "All that painting and cleaning. You two kids have a good time." She waves her hand in our direction, and I glance at Kip. I wasn't expecting to be *alone* alone. My cheeks burn hot.

"Are you sure?" I ask her. She nods. "Ford?" I whisper.

"No, darlin'." He laughs. "I need a nap. I'm not used to waking up so early."

"Looks like it's just you and me, Murph."

Oh Lord.

30

When we get to the marina, Kip leaves me on the dock while he grabs the keys for the boat, a cruiser with a big cuddy cabin, all smooth white fiberglass and crisp green trim. *Barbara Jean*, Kip's mom's name, written in fat cursive across the stern.

I sit on the vinyl seat next to the driver's and wait. From Back Creek, I look at my island. A duck lands in the marsh near Our Lady and dips its head in the shallow water.

"Ready?" Kip holds up the keys, and I gulp.

"Can you legally drive a boat?" I ask as he sits. "Don't you need a license?"

"Can you legally drive a sub?" he jokes, starting the engine. I know it's like a car, sixteen, and I'm a little nervous. My hands are sweating. *Barbara Jean* idles quietly.

"Your dad doesn't care if you take it?"

"No." He smiles. "Omar and I took it out when we were nine, and my mom was so angry, but they don't care now. Dad told me I could. Promise." He eases the boat from the dock and steers into the channel leading out to the Bay.

"Your dad doesn't hate me?"

"He thinks you make me less annoying." Kip laughs. "Now, my mom on the other hand . . ."

Kip follows the markers. I'm going to have to do the same thing, but underwater. My stomach rolls. I don't know if I can do it.

We start to go faster, the wind already whipping my hair around. I pull it into a ponytail so it doesn't get too enormous or smack Kip in the face. The noise from the motor and the wind lets me sit with my thoughts. I know, kiss or no kiss, this is the best birthday I've ever had.

Every few minutes, I look over at Kip, who is steering with a content look on his face. What's he thinking about? Does he think we're going to kiss? Does he want to?

I burrow deeper and deeper within my brain like a frog in mud, thinking it will take us hours to reach the opposite shore, but it takes less than half an hour. When Kip slows down, I realize we're only a few more minutes away.

"It looks just like our side," I say. It does. The shore is sandy, with seagrasses beyond, and leafy trees stretch overhead.

"What'd you expect? Palm trees? Coconuts?" He winks.

I look at my hands. "I don't know. I've never been." When I was little, I would ask my dad to take me with him.

Plenty of other kids go out on the boats. But he never let me. He said I would get hurt, so I haven't been to the Eastern Shore even though it's only seven miles away.

"Oh, Murph," he says. "I'm sorry. I won't make jokes for your birthday." He looks embarrassed. Like when he found me on the beach crying. It was months ago. Forever ago. "Well, now you're here." He stretches out his arms and gestures toward the shoreline.

Kip turns off the engine and stands, then drops the anchor. It's quiet, the water lapping the boat. "What do you want to do?" he asks.

My answer is kiss. He's standing over me, looking down. Yes, kiss. "I don't know."

"Do you want to leave?" He puts his hand to the back of his neck. "I know you don't like swimming."

"No!" I yell. *Relax, Murphy.* I breathe out slowly. "No," I say more normally. "Let's get shells for Babe." A pile of them are always on the counter at the marina.

"Okay, but my mom might murder her. She's been gluing them to everything in the house."

I smile. Kip pulls off his T-shirt, and I look away, then back again, trying to keep it together. Which is difficult. He balls up the shirt and throws it in his seat. Where exactly am I supposed to look? He leans on one arm and hops over the side, landing in the water. "Are you gonna stay in the boat?" he asks.

"No." I stand up and scowl. Even though I'm wearing a swimsuit, Lydia's red one-piece, I don't want to take my shirt off in front of him.

"You can use the cabin if you want." Kip points to the little room under the bow.

When I come back, he takes my hand and pulls me over the edge, his other hand on my waist. Oh Lord. The water is warm and shallow, and we stand like that for a lot longer than we need to.

But I'm still not ready, so I let go and walk up the beach, Kip behind me. I stay away from him, really as far as I can, which I know is weird. But I'm nervous. I collect a handful of shells, walk back to him, and drop them in the bucket.

My third time, Kip says, "Are you having fun? I don't want to ruin your birthday . . ."

I refuse to look at him. If anyone's ruining anything, it's me.

I take a deep breath and look him square in the eye. I'm so close, I could count each freckle. "I'm nervous," I blurt out. "I turned fourteen, and I've never kissed anyone." I cross my arms in front of my suit. "And I decided I want to kiss you."

"Okay," he says.

"Okay, like you want to kiss me too?"

"Yeah."

I pull on my red strap. My fingers are tingly. *Kip wants to kiss me too.* "Some people think Joan was in love with the married knight who sponsored her." I freeze when I repeat the words in my head. I am so embarrassing.

Kip keeps a straight face for exactly five seconds. "Did he look like me? Then I would understand. She definitely was, then."

I knew he would make jokes. "Can we stop talking, please?"

He nods, and it's very quiet. Seagulls caw behind me. His face is so close, I can feel him breathe. If I don't kiss him, I will die. I will melt and ooze into the Bay like oil. The fluttery feeling in my ribs gets bigger and bigger until I close my eyes and lean in.

I kiss Kip Dwyer on the mouth. And it is a little messy. But. It is starry nights on a bridge. And fireworks. Warm hugs on porches. It is floating and flying and drifting.

It is perfect.

31

"Tell me about it," Lydia demands two days later, the Friday night before my practice launch. One week before the real launch and Ford leaves for Japan. Lydia's editing her movie on her computer, her face a few inches from the bright screen. I'm lying on her bed.

"No. I don't make you talk about kissing Omar."

"Why not? That's what friends do."

"I don't want to." I'm afraid if I think about it too much, if the words come out, it will disappear. Like it never existed in the first place.

"It was that bad?" Lydia turns around with wide eyes.

"No, it wasn't bad at all. It was wonderful." I sigh and cover my face with a pillow covered in pink skulls. "I told him happy birthday afterward."

"Why? Isn't his birthday in March?"

"Yes!" I throw the pillow across the room and hit her in the butt, and my voice is no longer muffled. "Because I am not normal."

"For you, that's not that bad," she says, laughing. I don't mention the Joan thing.

"Can we eat?" Lydia stands up. "I'm hungry and need to take a break. This doesn't look how I want it to look." She flings her hands toward the computer.

"What's wrong with it?"

"It's not . . ." She purses her lips. "Inspired enough."

I don't know what that means. I raise my eyebrows. "Let's eat."

Saturday is practice for a practice. Practice in the driveway for Sunday's practice launch. For the last few days, I've learned how to open the oxygen tanks, tested out the motor in the large garbage bin filled with water, and manipulated the hand and foot controls.

Ford makes me sit in the sub in the morning, when it's cooler, for three hours, just to monitor the oxygen. Every thirty minutes, I open the valves and record the information. I check the carbon dioxide scrubber.

At the three-hour mark, Kip opens the hatch and peers down at me, his hair a fuzzy blond halo. "How was it?"

"Fine." I grab his hand, and he hoists me out. The freckles on his hand make me clear my throat and yank my hand back when I come out of the hull.

Ford's standing on the gravel. "How was the breathing?" He's in full military mode. No smiles with his bottom teeth. No dear. No honey.

"Okay," I say, wiping my forehead. "We need more silica gel. The fish finder fogged up." That will help me see where I'm going. So a boat doesn't run me over.

"Hmm, what were the numbers on that?" He crosses his arms, the sleeves rolled tight.

I push my hair into a ponytail. The Bay will be much cooler underwater. "I was fine. The lowest was eighteen percent." Lower than that, and I would start to feel funny. Dizzy.

"You won't feel so relaxed tomorrow."

I don't know what he wants from me. "I'll sing a song like you told me."

"If you feel faint or different in any way, you tell us over the radio immediately. Are you tracking?" I do have a backup to my oxygen, sulfate candles. They will release pure oxygen into the hull. Open flames are dangerous, but they are quick and effective if the tanks malfunction. Not enough to travel over miles, but enough to let me surface and open the hatch.

His nagging is annoying me. "I know, Ford." I rub my eye.

His face softens. Thankfully. "A lot of time to think down there, huh?"

"Too much. I'll start talking to myself." Obviously. I already had an hour-long chat with Joan.

"What were you thinking about?" Kip asks, grinning. "Anyone I know?"

I stare up at him, my eyebrows pushed down low. It's my best move. "The sub." Except for the hours I spent thinking about kissing.

"Okay, okay," he says, his arms surrendering. "Remember when you thought it was my birthday?"

"I hate you, Kip Dwyer." Except I don't. Not at all.

Ford steers me toward the cottage. "Let me get you some lunch, Mary, Mary, Quite Contrary. That will make you feel better."

∾∾∾∾∾∾∾∾∾∾∾∾∾∾∾∾∾∾∾∾∾∾∾∾

Sunday morning, I wake up early, my body stiff from hours cramped in the sub. I try to stretch the feeling back into my muscles. The house is quiet. In the bathroom, I stare at my serious reflection in the mirror.

I wet my brush under the tap and wrestle my hair. I need the security of my braids today. I part it down the center and make two neat French braids, pulling them tight so I can feel my heartbeat on my scalp.

"You're not going to let me die today, Joan, right?"

I pray.

I know Ford will have food, but before my nerves get the better of me, I attempt to eat a banana in the kitchen.

My mother walks in with coffee. We haven't talked since my birthday. I haven't told her what I'm doing or what today is. I don't plan to either.

"I checked your dad's pots and sold the crabs. Got a good price for the males."

I freeze. My mouth goes dry. An eerie feeling runs through me. I grip the counter in front of me. Money is always good news in the Murphy house, but I don't trust what it means this time. I dread the words that will come next.

"I've got enough for your dad's bail. I can pick him up tomorrow."

I was right.

My dad is coming home.

32

The bells from Our Lady ring as I walk over to the marina. Nuns file into the church, a black line on the pink horizon. I slip into the side chapel, little candles in red votives lining the wall in front of a statue of Mary.

I kneel on the leather stool and close my eyes. "He's coming home." I clasp my hands near my lips. "Mary." I don't know what to say at first. "I don't want him to."

Why did she have to tell me today? Why now? My thoughts are wild. Frantic. I shake my head. I can't think about him. I have to concentrate on the sub. On the launch.

I peek with one eye up at the saint. "I want to survive." I want to survive. I need to.

"I think I'm named after you." I pause. "Along with millions of other girls, but still. You're the Star of the Sea. Protect me. Please."

With twitching fingers, I light a candle and watch the little flame hover in the dark of the church. "Amen," I whisper.

Because of the tides, we push the launch back to eight, and I have time before the others come. I check on the sub, which they moved to the boathouse yesterday, and see it intact, *Murphy's Law*. Meet the bad luck head-on.

I hug my shoulders. To distract myself, I take out my checklist and reread it, then line up the contents of my backpack on the dock. I mentally match them to their job on the list, then repack my bag. When I'm done, I stand up and find my life preserver in the box of the Dwyers' supplies.

On the dock, I sit and wait, the life preserver tight on my ribs. Kip comes in a few minutes later.

"Hey," he says, sitting beside me. "Can you wear that?"

"No, I can't move with it. It'll be next to me." I just like the security of it. It's holding my insides together.

"Murph, I want to make a joke about you wearing it on land. But it's your day. No jokes."

No jokes from Kip makes me nervous. I look at his gap. He smells like toothpaste. "He's coming home tomorrow. My mom just told me." I thought I had time. Ten days. By that time, I'd have done it, piloted a sub across the Bay. Now I'm not so sure.

"What do you want to do?" Kip asks. He grabs my hand and sandwiches it between his and the dock.

"I don't know." An itchy despair creeps up my spine.

"Do you still want to do this?"

"More than anything." I stare at *Murphy's Law*. Mr. Dwyer and Ford tested the pressure hull by lowering it into the marina and bringing it back up manually, with no pilot. All the measurements were the same. No leaks.

"All right, lovies," Ford says, walking into the boathouse, "none of that. We've got a sub to launch."

Lydia shows up, complaining about how early it is, while I'm reciting the prelaunch checklist with Ford. Mr. Dwyer is here now too, waiting by a winch, his red hair and freckles bright. He wraps his big arms around Kip in a huggy, wrestling move.

"Let me know when you're ready," he tells me. He pretends to throw Kip in the water.

"You have everything?" Ford asks. "Remember, you're only staying in the marina this time. If you need us, radio over. We will haul you out or come down and get you."

I nod. I imagine the sub sinking to the bottom of the marina and seaweed creeping its way around the hull, a tangle so thick, no one will ever find me.

So much work. Weeks of work just to end up in the bottom of the marina. Just to end up in the same town. On the same island.

"Are you ready?" Ford asks. "Any last-minute nerves?"

"No. Once I set my mind to something, I do it."

"Give me a hug," Ford says. "Never said that to one of my submariners before." He squeezes me, his small body only slightly bigger than mine. I bite my lip and tell myself Joan probably didn't cry when she left for war.

"I need one too," Lydia interrupts. She latches on. "Don't die," she whispers. "I'm so glad we're friends again."

"Me too."

She puts her chin against my head. "I'm proud of you."

When it's Kip's turn, he says, "I'm not hugging you. Or saying good-bye." He stands in front of me, his shoulders square in his red shirt. For a minute, I don't want to climb in my sub. I want to stay on land where life is normal.

But tomorrow will be the normal I'm used to.

So today is the day life changes.

"Game face on, Murph. Let's go." Kip pats me gruffly on the back and steps to the winch.

They lower me into the water.

33

It's quiet inside the sub. So quiet that when I unzip my back-pack, the noise echoes around me. Flat on my stomach, I take out my flashlight first and place it on the bottom. Next, the radio. I switch it on so it hums.

I put Joan's card, found in my jumper pocket, above my hand controls, her halo golden. I kiss my fingertips and press it to the picture. I make the sign of the cross. I am not afraid. I am not afraid. *Please don't let me die. Please.*

I put my feet back by the rudder and diving plane con-trols. The sleeping bag Ford gave me separates my ribs from the metal.

Over the radio, Kip says, "If you're ready, we're going to unhook you."

I hold the button down. "Okay."

The sub lurches a little, and I brace myself with my elbows. The water cradles me for a second, then drops. I flip on the motor and pivot the ballast tanks.

"You're free," Kip says.

I don't feel free.

"I feel like we should say 'Over,'" he says.

"Are you a truck driver?"

"I do love gas station food. Over."

I smile. "I'm sure that won't get annoying."

"I'm never annoying. Ford is losing it, by the way. He's very worried about you. He's pacing up and down the dock, watching your buoy. Over."

Ford wants me close today. The bright orange bubble that open-water swimmers use for safety is tied to my hatch to track me. He wants me to sit in the sub and practice the controls. Not leave the safety of the marina water. Next week, I can leave the marina. But by next week, it will be too late.

That despair keeps sneaking in.

Joan wouldn't wait. Not if her life depended on it.

For twenty minutes, I stare out at the channel that leads across the Bay, that sinking feeling in my chest. In front of me, I see a trio of skates slide past my sub, their stomachs white. They flap under the wooden posts of the pier.

Kip says, "Mary?"

No "Murph." I frown. "Why no 'Over'?"

"The Coast Guard is here." I hear yelling. Muffled yelling. "I think Ford's getting in trouble."

I press my lips together. Because of me? I put my hand

on the ballast control. I could go up. The Coast Guard would take my sub. They might arrest me or Ford. And then what? I'd never get to pilot my sub.

Or. Or. I could go. I could flee. I could do what I was born to do.

"Kip." I lift my chin, my heartbeat pinging between my ribs and the sub. Ricocheting like a bullet. "Kip. You asked me what I wanted to do, and I know. I'm going to go across the Bay. Today. Can you get your boat to follow me?"

"Murph." So much reservation in one syllable. But he doesn't say "Mary." It's something. A chance.

"My dad is not going to let me do it, Kip. Okay? He's not. I need to go now. This is my only chance," I plead.

It's very quiet on the other end. Like he's not holding the button down. Either something happened or he's thinking. Or he's grabbing the boat. Whatever it is, it's probably bad. He's probably not going to help me escape.

I bite my thumbnail. "Kip!" I watch the fish finder, and the water is empty ahead of me through the narrow channel Kip took the *Barbara Jean* on my birthday.

Still nothing over the radio. Not even static.

I push my eyebrows down. "I'm going no matter what. Okay? So you can go with me or not."

On the other end, Kip curses. "I'm trying to sneak past the Coast Guard to get keys to help my girl. Could you please keep it down?"

I grin so hard it hurts. Kip Dwyer. If I could see his freckled face, I'd kiss it.

34

If I can survive steering through the narrow marina, the open water should be easier to navigate. My eyes dart between the compass on the outside of the porthole and my maps. I push the foot controls too hard and then too soft. Even though I've practiced for weeks, it's suddenly different.

"Relax, Murphy. Relax." I try again.

"There's a big ship at the mouth, do you see it?" Kip asks. "Over."

"I see it."

"Let it get by you. Over."

The sub sways under me. The wake from the ship. It makes me feel small, like a minnow compared to a whale. I press my elbows into the sleeping bag to steady myself. It does nothing. I hum to myself. The Our Lady song we sing in chapel once a week.

"I felt that," I tell Kip. "I didn't like it."

"I think that'll be the only one. The big ships are headed toward the ocean, not up the Bay. Over."

Following the maps, I start again, pushing the motor harder as I leave the marina. "I'm out."

The first hour is easy. The water gets deeper, the sub gets cooler, and I figure out the foot controls. I pull the sleeping bag up to my waist as I drive.

"I saw a bugeye," he says. The wooden oyster boat of the Bay. "Maybe our next project can be that or a skipjack. What do you say?"

I smile and press the pedals behind me.

"Halfway, Murph. Over."

Good. I have about two hours of oxygen left and an hour and a half to go. "Tell me about Ford and the Coast Guard. Do you think he got arrested?"

I can hear Kip laughing. "He was saying curse words I've never heard in my life. They took him somewhere, which was a good distraction. And Lydia's mad at me because I didn't take her with me. But she was on the other side of the boat-house! I couldn't get to her! Over."

"Thanks for coming with me." Kind of with me. Above me. I look up at the roof of the sub like I can see his boat.

"You're not getting mushy on me, are you?" There's static for a second. "Of course I would. You do things for your lady love."

I roll my eyes and beam at the same time. But to Kip, I say, "You forgot to say 'Over.'"

"You're heartless." I can practically see his gap through the radio. "I'll check in with you in five minutes. Over."

For the next thirty minutes, he checks in like he says. It's quiet when he leaves, and each time I miss a voice other than my own. I put the radio down and look through the porthole. I'm so far down, I can see only a few feet in front of me. A storm last week left the water murky. I've gone almost five miles in less than two hours. If I'm reading my maps correctly, I have two miles to go.

While he's gone, I open the valve to the oxygen and record the numbers.

"Time. You alive down there? Over."

"Yes, I'm two miles out. Does that match up with you?"

"Yeah. See you in five. Over."

Kip checks in five more times, and I run my finger over the path on the map. I'm going to do it. I'm going to cross the Bay in a submersible.

"Murph? Over."

"Here."

"How's life at the bottom of the sea? Over."

"Fine." I press the radio to my mouth, but it falls out of my hands and bangs against the metal side. "Whoops," I say aloud. My fingers feel funny.

"You can't say fine because that's what we say when we're not fine. So say a different word. Over."

"Okay." My fingers feel too big on the button. I look at the radio, confused, and blink. When I measure the oxygen levels, they're low. Really low. Fourteen percent. I don't want to tell him. He'll make me come up.

"Okay? Hey, stay on the radio for a minute. I want to make sure your oxygen is working."

"Slope hair fling." I shake my head. Which leaves my vision blurry. My words aren't working either. Or my hands. I try to hum.

"What, Murph? I didn't hear you. Over."

"Solry. Is fli herb." No. I am not working.

"Murphy?"

I can tell he's nervous. I'm nervous. My tongue is stuck, and I stare at the depth charts as the lines dance around. They dance even when I squint my eyes. *Stop moving, please.* I breathe, and my ribs move against the sub.

"Mary? Come up right now!" He's yelling at me. Kip doesn't yell at me. I reach for the radio. "Murphy!"

I fumble with the button again. "No." I am not stopping now. I'm so close. So very, very close.

"Listen. You're losing oxygen. Get up here!"

He doesn't say "Over." I want to tell him. I want to tell him I'm okay. That I'm just tired, and I can finish this no problem. But I'm not okay. I grab for my backpack, my hands like I'm wearing thick mittens.

"Murph. Please take a breath of real air." He curses, and I tune him out.

My mittened hands keep dropping the bag, and I can't hold on. I lie on my side for a minute, no idea where the sub is going.

I just want to sleep. My eyes blur, looking at the picture of Joan, and I close them. So wonderful. Joan did such a good job. I pull the sleeping bag up over my shoulders. It's so warm. So warm and comfortable.

The sub tilts and something hits me in the face. I push it away, but it hits me again. I groan and open my eyes. A sulfate candle. I gasp and push up.

35

I reach for the backpack again. This time, I get it, but my foot kicks the rudder behind me, lurching the sub to the side. I hold my breath and fumble to right it with my foot. My hands shake violently. I unzip the bag all the way and pull out the other candles and matches.

I light the match on my fourth try, the panic a stack of discarded sticks next to me.

Carefully, I place the candle on the map, trying not to let the flame devour the paper. My fingers won't stop vibrating.

"Okay," I say into the radio.

"Oh my God, you're alive. Are you coming up?"

I should. I really should. "No." I breathe the oxygen candle fumes in, my nose an inch away from the flame. I feel better, still foggy, but better.

"No, no, no, Murph. You're so close. Just come up."

I let his voice bounce around the sub while I line up the compass and map. I steered off course fifty yards. I'm north of our charted route. I tell him over the radio.

"You've got less than a mile until you ground. Over."

I sigh. "I'm okay," I tell myself and Kip. All I have to do is survive for a little longer, maybe thirty minutes, and I will make it. The candle flickers below me.

"You're not coming up?" I hear him sigh. "Okay, Murph."

"Here we go," I whisper.

I pull on the handle for the ballast tanks, and the sub rises. The depth charts say the water is twenty feet deep. The smaller the number, the closer I am, until the sub is waist-deep and I can open the hatch.

For the next twenty minutes, I lie frozen in the sleeping bag. The flicker of the flame makes me feel like I can't move. Kip checks on me constantly, and it's hard to concentrate.

At ten feet, the sub jolts, and I cry out. I must have hit something. Sand maybe. The shoreline. But I'm scared.

I yank on the ballast handle to raise the sub, but nothing happens. I'm stuck.

"Oh no, oh no, oh no." I speak, and the words make the flame flicker. I stare down and hold my breath. Please don't vanish. Please don't go out. But the flame wavers, then disappears, and five thousand thoughts explode in my brain.

I don't know where the matches are. I can't find them. I must have thrown them earlier. I turn the backpack over, empty it out, and run my hands over the supplies. Nothing. They're gone.

I sob and wipe my face. I suck in air, but there's nothing. No oxygen. It's like opening my mouth underwater and sucking in water. It's like drowning.

I swipe my eyes again and think. I can do this. If I can open the hatch, I can swim to the surface. It's not that far. I might be so close. Or I might drown. I just learned how to float. And my body is tired.

I push myself up to the hatch and put my hands on the handle. The metal Mr. Jack welded is cold. I tighten my muscles and get ready. I know there will be a rush of water. My biceps shake.

Do I let it fill up and then leave? Or swim right away? I can't remember. I can't remember what Ford told me. What his book said. I cry out and close my mouth.

Get it together, Murphy. Get it together. Push open this hatch and go. Swim.

I close my eyes, clench my fingers around the handle, and lean against the side. I twist and push. Nothing happens. My heart pumps hard in my chest. I can do this. I have opened the hatch before. I steady my hands again.

I twist and push. Again, nothing happens.

I can't do it.

I try again.

Tears stream down my face, and I let them. I stop and lie on my sleeping bag, my face to the hatch. I can't do it. I was so close. *Don't give up. Just rest your eyes.* Just for a second. To gather my thoughts. Then I can try again. Swim up. To the bobbing light of the sun.

I shut my eyes and put my hands to my heart.

Just a second. That's all.

36

The hatch opens, and I blink into the blinding light.

I'm not underwater. I'm in the sky. The bright blue sky. I squint. Wings. White wings, larger than the body attached. Each feather is bigger than my hand. So soft. I could touch one. Touch one of the feathers and float away.

"Mary." The voice is far away, drifting above me. "Give me your hand."

A red dress. Short hair. Serious face. The sun glows around her. I smile. She is so beautiful. "Joan."

"Take a breath."

I nod. I am not afraid. I will breathe for Joan of Arc.

"No, really. Do it." She waits for me, her hand extended. "Give me your hand. I can't reach you." She touches her fingers to mine. They're a lot bigger than I expected. And freckled.

"Your hand looks like a boy's," I tell her.

"Makes sense." The hand reaches down farther. "I can't fit in there. Please. You are my favorite person in the world, but help me out. Please come up."

"No, Joan." I roll over and put my head under the sleeping bag.

"Murph, give me your hand!"

I stop smiling and yank off the sleeping bag. "Kip?"

"Who else would it be? Let's go."

I grab his hand, and he pulls me out of the hatch. I look around and gasp like I've been under the water for three hours, which I have. The sun glints off the water, warm on my face. "Should I kiss the beach?"

He laughs. "I'd rather you kiss *me*, but you can do whatever you want."

The beach is twenty-five yards away from us, the waves lapping against the boat. "I did it," I tell him.

"You did," Kip says. We're sitting on top of the sub, my feet near the stenciled name. "I knew you could, but yeah . . ." He jumps into the water. "Do you think you can make it to the boat?"

"I just piloted a sub across the Bay. Yes, I can wade twenty feet to the boat." My legs are wobbly, and I almost fall, but I don't want to admit it. When I get to the stern, I stop. I won't be able to make it up the ladder by myself. "Okay, I know what I just said, but I need help. My body isn't working." I frown.

He smiles and pretends like I'm a pain, pulling me up. Using the side as a railing, I walk slowly to the front seat.

"Can you call Lydia? She's been texting me every minute." He hands me a towel, and I wrap it around my legs.

I shiver while he dials. When he hands me the phone, I hear a squeal. "You did it? You're alive?"

She's so loud, I have to hold it away. "Barely. But yes." I'm grinning and dancing my feet on the bottom of the boat.

"Yay! We need to celebrate! Kip thought you were dead, so I needed to hear your voice."

I put the phone down. "Did you think I was dead?"

"I did." He touches his sunburnt neck and smiles. "Did you think I was Joan of Arc?"

I pinch my eyes shut. "Maybe."

"Well, that's ridiculous because she was definitely not as good-looking as me."

I make a face. But it's not real. Not at all.

Kip leans close and puts his hand on mine. "If anything, you're like her."

I raise my eyebrows. "Not good-looking?"

He shakes his head. "No, strong." He squeezes my hand and starts the engine. Kip turns the boat toward Bournes, and I smile bigger than I ever have in my life.

While we head home, I know, now more than ever, that I can't go back to my old normal.

Grieving Joan of Arc, the French people fought harder for their freedom. And twenty-two years after her death, the English left France for good. King Charles demanded a retrial for the girl who made him king.

Because the unfair trial had happened in the Church courts, the king needed help. He needed the Church to take responsibility. Joan's pope had passed away, and a new pope, Nicholas V, wanted a strong relationship with the new France.

Two of the men who had sentenced Joan to death were also deceased, but the remaining churchmen were interviewed and given amnesty. They wouldn't be punished for what they had said about Joan's case.

They agreed that the trial had been political. That it was meant to make it look like Charles had been crowned by a witch.

They interviewed childhood friends and soldiers about Joan. One hundred and fifteen people told her story. How she was brave and loyal. How she prayed. How she was honest and truthful. Many people admitted they had lied at the earlier trial.

Twenty-five years after her death, the first trial was declared flawed.

France rejoiced.

Four hundred years after her death, she was nominated for sainthood. And finally, in 1920, Joan became Saint Joan of Arc. Just like her idols who had spoken to her in her father's garden.

37

As soon as I get to Bournes, my feet on solid ground, I call
Betty on the phone she bought me and ask her if she and
Alex would meet me for dinner. She says of course.

At the Harbor, we sit at a table far from the bar, but the
crowd is loud, and bursts of laughter echo around us.

Alex is quiet. She hugs me, and her long black hair tick-
les my nose. She pats my hand when we sit. When our drinks
come, Betty squeezes a lemon into her water and stirs it with
a spoon.

"How was the practice launch?" she asks.

I fidget. "It wasn't a practice exactly. I crossed the Bay."

"You what?" Betty leans forward and looks over her
glasses at me.

I tell them all about it, a thrill building in my chest as I
recount the morning. Alex clasps her hands together, and her

pretty silver bracelets clink when she moves her wrist. By the time I'm finished, I can't remove the smile from my face. I did it. I piloted the sub. My sub.

"Perhaps your submersible could do a world of good for our waterways. Exploring and discovering," Alex says. "How very courageous of you."

"It made me realize something," I say. I tip my chin up, but my fingers fiddle with my fork. "Mom is picking up Dad tomorrow."

Alex and Betty look at each other.

"I don't want . . . I don't think it's good for me to live with him. I was thinking about what you and Mr. Harris said . . ." I know she's offered, but this is harder than I thought.

I've never felt like I belonged anywhere, but I do now. I belong to Betty and Ford and Lydia and Kip. All these wonderful people who wanted to be part of me. My family.

"Could I live with you?" I manage.

Betty smiles with crinkly eyes. "We were hoping that's what you wanted to talk about," she says. "Your mother and I wanted it to be your decision. No one wanted to pressure you."

Alex puts her hand on mine, the silver bracelets knocking together when they touch my skin. "We would love that."

I close my eyes in relief. "And I understand I'll have to go to school in North Beach instead of Our Lady." I say it, but I choke a little. I could see Kip and Lydia on the weekends probably. And holidays.

"Oh, honey," Betty says. "Where do you want to go to school?"

I tell her the truth. "Our Lady."

"Then you'll go to Our Lady, Mary."

~~~~~~~~~~~~~~~~~~~~~~~~~~~~~~~~~~~~~

Mr. Harris is surprised to hear my voice. I ask him to meet me at the library in the morning. Then I crawl under the covers and sleep in the house on Bleecker Street for the last time.

In the morning, Betty picks me up just like usual, like nothing is different. Only, everything is different. At eight, Mr. Harris walks into the library with his red nylon bag, and we sit in the conference room used for story time with the toddlers.

I tell him everything, every hit and bruise, and he writes it down in my case file. Each word leaks out, and instead of leaving me empty, it fills me up. I feel brave and strong. I feel more like Joan of Arc than ever.

Mr. Harris drafts a safety plan. I will move into Betty and Alex's house on Tuesday, tomorrow. Tonight, I will sleep at Lydia's to say good-bye.

Betty drops me off at my best friend's house and hugs me tight. When I walk in, Lydia sprints down the stairs. "It's finished!" she yells. "It's finished!"

"Let's watch it," I say.

"Well, it's only fifteen minutes long, so I want to stretch

it out. I'll make popcorn." She calls out the window to her parents. "Mom, where is the popcorn?"

"In the pantry."

"Why are you both in swimsuits in our front yard? It's gross! The neighbors don't want to see that!"

I don't hear what her mother says because I'm laughing. When we have our popcorn in a bowl and cold sodas, we go upstairs and sit on her unmade, rumpled bed, the sheets with gold crowns.

"I haven't uploaded it yet, so if you see something terrible, please tell me. But gently. I am a very tender human."

"Okay." I fold my legs under me and put the popcorn in my lap. Lydia pulls her laptop over, presses play, and stares at me while the movie plays.

The dragon keeps scorching the village. It does it over and over. When the villagers repair their houses, when they replant the beautiful flowers, the dragon swoops in and terrorizes again. It steals a human.

Repeatedly, the girl watches her village get destroyed. She weeps and feels powerless.

But the dragon steals a glimmering heart gem. A red heart in the middle of the charcoal town. The dragon flies away, and the girl stops crying. She finds a sword in the rubble.

Armed with the sword, the girl journeys. She finds the dragon in the cave. She tiptoes around it while it sleeps, a concerned look on her face. When it wakes, the dragon sees the girl and rears back, its neck long and scaled.

Fire spews from its mouth, singeing the girl's dress.

She raises her sword high, and my heart pounds. Lydia didn't want to kill the dragon. "What's going to happen?" I ask, gripping the popcorn bowl.

The dragon shoots fire again, and the girl plunges the sword into the white, scaly stomach.

Instead of slinking down in pain, the dragon becomes hundreds of little yellow flower petals. They fall gently around the girl like rain.

Lydia slams the laptop shut. "It's so bad."

"It's not bad. It's perfect." I pry the computer back open.

"It's not. It's awful. I can't even watch it."

"Lydia Anderson, it was the most beautiful, perfect movie I've ever seen in my life. You're amazing." I hug her close.

"Sometimes dragons need to be slayed," she says.

I nod against her. "Sometimes dragons need to be slayed."

38

I lie next to her until it's late. Until it's after midnight. I can't sleep. I keep seeing the destruction the dragon left and how the girl had no choice.

When Lydia is asleep on the pillow next to me, I pull off the covers. Lydia wouldn't understand. And even though I'm telling her everything now, this is one thing I can't. She would be a good friend and want me to stay safe. She would tell me that it was just a story, that you shouldn't actually confront dragons. Which is true. I would tell myself the same.

But I sneak out of her house and walk through the dark to the house on Bleecker Street. I wait at the kitchen table. I don't know when he'll be home. Sometimes it's early, sometimes it's late. I prop my head on my wrist and wait.

I must fall asleep, because headlights in the window and the tires on the gravel wake me up. He's home. I rub my eyes and sit up straight.

He opens the door and walks toward the refrigerator. The greasy, smoky scent of the Tavern hits my nose as he passes me. He doesn't notice I'm here. I prepare myself and push my shoulders back.

I am not afraid.

"Hi, Dad."

He turns from the refrigerator to face me. "I didn't see you," he says, a chicken leg in his hand. His voice says he's functional. He will not fall asleep in his truck tonight. He will sleep in the bedroom at the end of the hall. Next to the room that used to be mine.

I am not afraid.

"I know what you did." My voice is strong. Stronger than his. I stand up.

"What are you talking about?" He's not angry yet. He might think he outsmarted me before. That a broken sub would keep me quiet. Keep me here. He's wrong.

I am not afraid.

"I talked to the social worker. I'm leaving."

"Good." He gives me something that looks like a smile. "Have fun with those girls."

His tone makes me cringe. "You need to do something first."

"I don't owe you anything." It's a sneer. He owes me everything. He owes me the world. My dad comes close to me and pushes, but I'm ready with planted feet, hands clenched at my side. He's predictable. His moves are the same every time, and I am prepared.

I take a step back and watch him stumble to the side. "You do. You owe me sixty dollars for the broken glass on my sub. I worked hard for that money."

He pushes his hair to the side and spits when he speaks. "I'm not giving you that."

I am not afraid.

"Give me the money or I'm telling them in court." His mouth hangs open, and a piece of chicken skin clings to his lip. "I talked to a lawyer today. He told me if I press charges, you'll be in jail for a year."

He curses at me, his face brilliant red, inches from mine. He lifts his fist, but I stand still, my chest out.

I am not afraid.

"If you do that, it'll be five years," I say.

I leave the house and steady myself against the wall. My hands shake beside my legs like fishing lines trembling with life. I take deep gulps of air and close my eyes. I stood up to him. I stood up to my dad. I've never done that before. And I lied too. I don't even know a lawyer.

In the morning, after breakfast with Lydia's family, Mr. Harris makes arrangements for me to pack up my room while my dad is out on the water. I find sixty dollars on my desk. Betty sits in the kitchen talking with my mother while I sort my life into boxes. Uniforms packed into brown cardboard.

While I'm folding a jumper, my mom walks in and stands in the doorway.

I keep my eyes on the plaid. The fabric is more faded than ever, but I'm sure these will stay packed or be donated. Betty will buy me new uniforms for ninth grade. Sister Bridget won't be able to yell at me.

"It's better," my mom says.

I smooth the dress down against my legs and pick at a piece of lint. "What is?"

"If you live with Betty. She'll take care of you," she says quietly in the doorframe.

My stomach wobbles.

She pushes her hair back. "I have something for you." She holds a small, wrapped box. "For your birthday. I'm sorry it's late."

Before I take it, I look at her face. She looks tired. I know she's been working a lot and setting Dad's crab pots while he was gone. I put the box in my palm and unwrap the paper. Folded inside white slippery fabric is a little gold medal. I take it out and hold it up gingerly. Joan of Arc. Etched and delicate.

"Thank you." I can't remember her ever getting me something like this. The saint holds her sword high.

"I know I'm no Betty, but I think I still know you pretty well."

I open my mouth to reply, but no words come out. What am I supposed to say? I blink and bite my lip. "You could come too, Mom. You could leave him."

Her shoulders drop. Like they've carried so much for so long. And I wait for her to say she'll come with me.

"It's not that easy," she says.

Her hair trails behind her when she leaves.

39

When I'm all packed, Betty drives me to North Beach, to her trim, one-story rambler with yellow flowers in the front yard. I stand in the driveway and survey my new house. I'm scared. And excited. Will I make new friends? Will I see Kip and Lydia as much?

The inside is clean and efficient with smooth wood floors and sunny windows. My room is white, for now, but Betty lets me pick out blue paint. A dresser matches a twin bed, and a poster of a submarine is pinned to a bulletin board. World War II's USS *Tautog*.

"I know it doesn't look like yours, but that's what I found online." She adjusts her glasses. "I'm sorry that's all there is."

"Thank you, Betty, for everything." I could say it every minute for the rest of my life, and it still wouldn't be enough. I pat the poster. "This sub sank the most enemy ships in World War Two."

"You know a lot about submarines," Betty says. She sits on the bed. "How are you feeling about your mom?"

I pull on my ear and shove my hands in my pockets. I don't know how I feel about her. Does she love me? Wouldn't she want me to stay with her, then? Wouldn't she leave my dad if she loved me? It's almost like we're strangers.

"I wish she'd leave him." I wish she had tried harder to go.

Betty pushes against her glasses. "Adults are confusing. We make decisions that maybe we don't even understand. I think she should leave him too, but it's not up to us. Your mother's been in that house for a long time. And change is hard."

Change is hard. I learned that even though I didn't want to. But change can also be wonderful.

On Saturday, Kip asks me to meet him at the Cliffs at exactly 11:45. Which is strange. But Alex drops me off close to the entrance, and I follow the shore, my shoes heavy in the soaked sand. I stand beneath the grainy mountains. I might not see them as much now. But I don't need them like I used to.

"Hey," Kip says, walking toward me. "Where have you been all my life, Murph?"

"I didn't see you for one day." But it feels like it's been longer, so I move a little closer to him.

"You're still going to Our Lady, right?" he asks.

"Still going to Our Lady."

Kip reaches into the pocket of his sweatshirt. Our Lady Starfish on the chest. "I got you something. It's stupid . . . I wanted to give it to you before your trip, but you had to be an outlaw about that." He hands me a rabbit foot keychain.

"Oh," I say. It's white. I can feel the bones through the fur, which grosses me out.

"Can't a guy give a girl a dead animal foot? Isn't it the most romantic thing anyone has ever done for you?"

It is.

Rubbing the back of his neck, he laughs and says, "I know it's a bad present, but my grandpa gave it to me for a Little League game, and we won. So I carry it around for luck." He looks at it in my hand, then brings his eyes up to mine. "Not that you need luck now. But so you remember your very handsome boyfriend."

"I will see you every day. Every single day, Kip."

"So you're saying I'm your boyfriend?" He can't grin any bigger. It would be impossible.

"Maybe it's not you, maybe it's a different boy." I am such a liar. But I can't keep a straight face either.

"Why are you so mean to me?"

I grin and look down at the white puff in my hand. "I carry a Joan card, for luck." Carried. It's pinned on the board in my new bedroom now. "Now this." I pull out the medal my mother gave me for him to see, and he leans in close.

Kip smells like gasoline and laundry detergent, which are probably not normal things to find attractive. But I do.

"I haven't heard a Joan fact in a long time." He's quiet and close. Very close.

I scrunch up my face, and my ears are hot. "She knew she was going to die, but she went on her quest anyway."

"A lot darker than I expected, Murph." Kip pulls me to him, and I wrap my arms around his waist. Is it possible to love someone's bones? If so, I love Kip Dwyer's bones. I bring my mouth up to his to kiss. We're better at it this time.

Kip breaks away and puts his face on the top of my head, his lips near my hair. "Always trying to make out, Murph. I swear. Would you please keep your hands off me? We've got places to go."

I roll my eyes, then push away from him. "Where?"

"Ford's for lunch!"

~~~~~~~~~~~~~~~~~~~~~~~~~~~~

We walk back to the cottages, holding hands. Every time I peek over at Kip, his entire face winks back at me. "Everyone wants to say good-bye, okay? Even though it's only a twenty-minute drive to North Beach."

Good-byes. Instead of dread, I feel grateful.

At Ford's, two tables are set outside. Light tablecloths flutter in the breeze. Maybe twenty people are here. Lydia's parents and the Dwyer family. Betty and Alex. They wave to me. Ford and Lydia are placing silverware at white plates. When he spots me, Ford stops and puts his hands on his hips. We haven't spoken since the launch.

"This is for me?" I ask him.

"It is, even though you almost got me arrested, my dear." He doesn't look mad though. He's smiling and talking in his happy voice. "Luckily, I was merely detained for a few hours."

"I'm sorry," I tell him. "I had to."

"I suspect you did," he says. He drops his arms, then wraps them around me. "I'm proud of you. Not for disregarding orders, but for completing your journey and standing up for yourself. It's been a joy to watch you grow."

Those words cause my heart to lurch in the nicest way. I hug him tighter. I'm going to miss him when he leaves for Japan in a few days. "Thank you, Ford. For everything."

"Let's eat," he says, patting me on the back. "But tomorrow we need to go pick up your sub. I had my friend pull it up on his property. I told him my protégé made a reckless decision."

I spot Betty and Alex and bring them over to meet the man who helped me build and pilot a sub. While they talk, I pull away and find Lydia. She's wearing a flowered dress. I don't really have to say good-bye to her, but I do need to thank her.

"Thank you for pushing me and for making things beautiful," I say. "I'm so glad we're friends again."

"Best friends." She squeezes my hand.

Everyone sits, and Kip yells, "Sit next to me, Murph!"

I sit in a folding chair next to him. Without Kip, I wouldn't have survived science. Or the Murphy house. Or the trip across the Bay. From his left, he takes a tray of stuffed ham sandwiches, puts three on his plate, and passes the rest to me.

While he's eating, I say, "You made me believe in myself."

Kip stops chewing and winks at me.

"I told you to stop that winking business," I say.

Kip swallows and says, "I was eating! It was my only option!"

I smile and pick my own sandwich. I pass the tray along. I fill my plate as macaroni and cheese and cornbread and greens come down the line. All these people were not my family a few months ago, and now they are. All I had to do was let them in.

I start to tear up, and I clear my throat. All these people care about me.

I eat my food and listen to Ford tell the story about the Coast Guard, and Mr. Dwyer joins in. Everyone laughs. My heart swells.

Then it's time for dessert, and Ford brings out something chocolaty and wonderful, his pants rolled up like the first day I met him.

"To Mary!" he says. "To her voyage! Even though she disregarded orders." He smiles though.

Everyone looks at me. "Thank you for coming," I say. "Even though it seems a little silly to celebrate me."

Lydia shakes her head and laughs. But then everyone is laughing and talking again, and I can eat my cake in peace. The happiest I've ever been.

When it's time to leave, and I've hugged everyone good-bye, Betty pushes up her glasses. She's holding Alex's hand.

"Are you ready to go home?"

Home. I tip my face up and smile.

"I'm ready."

Author's Note

Mary's home life is partly inspired by my husband's experience as a social worker. Like Mary, kids are often scared of telling him about the abuse in their homes. They are scared of the unknown. They are scared of foster care. And sometimes, kids want to protect their parents. They love their parents despite everything.

Mary is hesitant to leave her family throughout most of the book because they are all she knows. It is her normal. I expect, to some readers, Mary's reluctance to tell Mr. Harris about what is happening at home is confusing. It seems so clear-cut, because the social worker only wants to help. But victims of domestic violence don't always see it this way.

Social workers don't want to take children away from parents. They want a child to be safe. Sometimes this means at home, and sometimes this means at another, safer home.

If you are experiencing abuse, you have options.

1. Tell a teacher or trusted adult. Teachers, social workers, nurses, doctors, police officers, and other educators are all mandated reporters. That means they are required by law to contact child protective services or child welfare agencies if

you are experiencing abuse or neglect. Child protective services must investigate each report. They can make a safety plan with you.

2. You or an adult can call the Childhelp National Child Abuse Hotline: 1-800-4-A-CHILD (1-800-422-4453).

3. If no one listens or helps, try a different adult. Call again. Don't give up. Everyone deserves to feel safe.

While I wanted to make the abuse reflect real-life circumstances, this is still a story. Mary makes an unsafe decision to confront her father. Mary followed the right steps earlier by contacting Mr. Harris, but confronting an abuser is not safe. I'm sure Lydia would have tried to talk her out of it.

Submarine and Submersible Resources

Real kids have built amazing submersibles! Mary and Kip build their own remote-controlled submersible, and then a real sub that Mary pilots, from videos on YouTube and Ford's book. They have a mentor who helps guide the dangerous undertaking. If you are interested in underwater and marine engineering, here are some available resources. Adult supervision is recommended.

SeaPerch is an underwater robotics program partnered with the U.S. Navy. Students in school or out-of-school teams build their own underwater robot and compete nationally. The website Seaperch.org has a list of established chapters, but teachers and mentors can apply for their own team too.

Ford's book is based on the manual I used for researching *Mary Underwater*. *Manned Submersibles* by R. Frank Busby is available online through the Biodiversity Heritage Library. The manual teaches you how to build a submersible and can be accessed at archive.org/details/mannedsubmersibl00busb.

Psubs.org is an online community of amateur sub builders and underwater explorers. Questions are asked and answered on the online forums.

Psubs.org is an online community of amateur sub builders and underwater explorers. Questions are asked and answered on the online forums.

If you are more interested in viewing others build a sub, you can check out the progress of Deep Sea Submarine Pisces VI on Facebook at facebook.com/piscessub. The sub is intended to be used for research and film.

Subnautica and *Subnautica: Below Zero* are survival video games by Steam. Players can collect submersibles and explore underwater terrain. More information can be found at Subnauticagame.com.

Acknowledgments

Mary Underwater would not exist without John Doleski's constant support. Thank you for believing I could write a book and get it published. For letting me steal time away from three babies to create. For listening to the same chapter over and over again. And for lifting me up when I floundered in rejection. This book is half your heart.

To my three babies, June, Teddy, and Dwyer, without you, I wouldn't have wanted to share my words. You give me a voice and a direction that I was severely lacking before you came into this world.

I am forever grateful to my agent, Veronica Park, for championing Mary Murphy in every iteration of her story. I knew we were kindred spirits when you called her a grumpy Anne Shirley.

To my editor at Amulet, Erica Finkel, thank you for seeing what this book could be. You are brilliant and insightful, and I will always be in shock that this is real. You really bought my Chesapeake Bay book and made it gleam like the inside of an oyster shell.

Many thanks to the rest of the team at Amulet and Abrams, especially Hana Anouk Nakamura, Amy Vreeland, Jenn Jimenez, Andrew Smith, Jody Mosley, Melanie Chang, Jenny Choy, Patricia McNamara O'Neill, Elisa Gonzalez,

Michael Jacobs, Emily Daluga, and Sara Sproull. Your hard work is wholly appreciated.

When I told my friends on Facebook that I planned on writing a book during Lent 2015 (Mary would approve), so many people encouraged me. To you all, you have no idea how much I needed those words. And special thanks to Jon VanDeventer and Stephen Balinski for answering STEM and submarine and Chesapeake Bay questions.

To Andrea Janes and Dr. Rita Pollard, the first to read my words, I am grateful for your kindness and encouragement.

To my critique partner, Amanda Fazzio, you have been a great friend and confidante during this publishing journey, and I am so glad we've shared it together. Jaye Robin Brown, thank you for your guidance and friendship. Mary is better because of both of you. Also, all of my fiery retreat friends, I am lucky to have you. Jen Malone, your mentorship has been so wonderful.

To my fellow 2020 debuts, especially the most parched, I am so lucky to share this experience with you. Prerna Pickett and Jenny Elder Moke, aren't I lucky to have met you?

The Weaver family, thank you for inviting us to dinner on the Bay. For planting the seed for this story. And for your early reading. No, you could not swim across the Bay, Tom, unless you trained.

My Joan of Arc research started when I was a middle schooler, but for *Mary Underwater*, *Joan of Arc*, a DK biography by Kathleen Kudlinski, was instrumental.

John Mayer, your song "Walt Grace's Submarine Test, January 1967" sparked this book when I was homesick for Maryland. To my former students and swimmers, who inspired Mary and Kip, I am so happy I was your teacher in that special place on the Bay.

And finally, I started writing stories when I was a little human. Lois and Steve Young are to blame. Thank you for letting me daydream. And for letting me believe I could be Joan of Arc. To my brother, Nate, and my sister-in-law, Catalina, I will talk about storytelling all night long with you.

And to my readers, I hope you know you are worthy. You are worthy just like Mary.

About the Author

Shannon Doleski was born and raised in Cazenovia, New York. After graduating from Niagara University with a degree in English education, Shannon was a high school and middle school teacher and swim coach in New York and Maryland. She lives in West Texas with her husband, three children, and beagle. *Mary Underwater* is her debut novel. Visit her author website at shannondoleski.com.